LOVING A PRINCESS

HER ROYAL BODYGUARD
BOOK 2

MARGAUX FOX

1

Erin knew she needed to get ready for the charity function, but she wasn't in a rush. She was lying in only her underwear on the big, four-poster bed with Audrey stretched out beside her, and she couldn't quite believe how her life had changed over the past few months. She ran her fingers over Audrey's big floppy ear. The fawn-coloured fur was as smooth as velvet. Audrey snored lightly. Although she was getting so big that her long legs took up at least half the bed, the pup had yet to fill out into her adult self. Erin smiled to herself. It felt crazy that this was her home now and that these luxurious surroundings weren't just somewhere she was working.

She looked across the room at the big window facing out onto the vast country estate. The winter sunlight was low in the sky and the sweet sound of absolute peace surrounded her. She could hear the water as Alex showered in their bathroom but otherwise, Erin appreciated the relative peace the castle offered in the early evening. Alex liked the staff to finish early and leave whenever possible. Both women appreciated their privacy.

Tonight would be their first night out together publicly as a couple, and they knew that half the world's media was desperately awaiting the appearance of the future queen of Great Britain and her new girlfriend.

If Erin allowed herself to think about it too much, it absolutely terrified her. She had been out with the princess before and had been photographed with her, of course. But that was as her bodyguard, as her shadow, as the grey woman in the background—while Alexandra dazzled and seduced. This would be different. Oh, so different.

The past couple of months since Alexandra's public coming out had been a whirlwind. Losing her role as Alex's bodyguard and secret love, and adjusting to the role of the princess's girlfriend, had shaken Erin more than she had ever imagined.

What had she dreamed it would be like? Had she really thought about it properly? Erin knew she hadn't. Not really. She'd had no real concept of what it would be, to be the girlfriend of one of the most famous women in the world, and she still didn't.

Erin only knew that she loved Alex. She had first met her as Princess Alexandra—so beautiful, so kind, and filled with compassion—yet so guarded. Then gradually, as time went on, Erin had realized the absolute privilege of knowing her privately, and then intimately.

At every new moment, Erin had loved her more.

She knew it had been a process for Alex to become herself over the past year, and this was still ongoing. Coming out, initially only to Erin and then recently to the whole world's media, had changed everything for her. Knowing Alex as she did now, Erin couldn't even imagine what it would have been like if Alex had kept that heavy secret and married a man, because that was the weight of expectation upon her.

Alex seemed so much freer and happier in herself since that press conference over the summer. She seemed cautious about the future sometimes, her blue eyes lost deep in thought—as though she still wasn't quite sure of the aftershocks of her "revelation." As though she worried that ripples from her announcement might be far-reaching and yet unknown.

So far, they had been far-reaching but mostly positive. Alex was receiving so much fan mail from women all over the world who were so grateful to her for coming out. What she received had been filtered by the staff, but Alex chose to read a good deal of it and to share it with Erin. Erin loved Alex's passion as she read these letters. She would sit with her feet up on the window seat in their bedroom in her silk lounge pants and a loose-fitting silk top, silhouetted against the lazy sunlight, and wade through piles of letters. Erin loved to see the fire in Alex's eyes when she would read one out to Erin. Alex was born to be a public face, and being able to use her fame for good and become a role model for the LGBT+ community was giving her a renewed sense of purpose.

Erin sometimes worried about her own purpose and what it was now—if she even had one, other than to be Alex's girlfriend. Loving and caring for Alex, she could do, but Erin worried that eventually she would need something more in her life.

The noise from the shower stopped, and Erin heard Alex drying herself and padding around the bathroom. The bathroom door opened and Alex emerged in a cloud of steam, wrapped in a fluffy white towel robe that, like most things, was oversized on her small frame.

Erin smiled when she saw her. She continued to be blown away by Alex. Her energy was so powerful, even stripped down from her public "princess persona" like this.

Alex's ash blonde hair was wet and looked much darker than usual combed back from her face, grazing her collarbones. Her face was fresh and bright, and scrubbed clean. It was rare that Alex's skin was free from makeup, and Erin loved to see her like that. Her eyes were such a dark, glimmering blue, like sapphires.

"Hey, Lover." Alex padded over to the side of the bed, her voice like liquid silk. Her eyes met Erin's.

"So, I was thinking," Alex continued, and her robe fell slightly open, revealing her breasts. She didn't move to hide them. Instead, she leaned in and kissed Erin, and Erin felt shivers run right through her body.

Alex's eyes twinkled with naughtiness as she reached into the bedside table and pulled out Erin's dildo and harness. "You could put this on . . . and I could take my robe off, and I think we have about twenty minutes before Alicia will be here for hair and makeup."

Erin laughed, but held her gaze. "Oh, you are nothing if not romantic, Princess Alexandra."

Erin pulled at the belt of Alex's robe, releasing it, and it fell open to reveal Alex's naked body. Erin never grew tired of looking at Alex. Her face, her body, dressed or undressed—she was always beautiful. Erin ran her hand down over Alex's hipbone, now gently covered in more supple padding. Alex had seemed less stressed since coming out, and her body seemed healthier for it.

Alex took hold of Erin's underwear at her hips and pulled. Erin raised her hips slightly to assist her, as her underwear slid down over her legs and off over her feet. Alex casually discarded Erin's sporty underwear and then picked up the black leather harness. Her elegant fingers worked to slightly loosen the straps on the harness. She put a hand on Erin's ankle and moved her right leg to the side of the bed, followed by her left leg, and Erin sat up on the edge of the bed, still smiling and letting Alex continue. Alex knelt on the carpet at Erin's feet and slipped the harness over each of her feet, pulling it up to her knees.

"So, because we don't want to disturb a snoring Audrey, I was thinking you should pull this up and then maybe take me to that big padded window seat." Alex stood up, walked to the window, and dropped the blinds—just in case—before slipping the robe off her shoulders. It fell to the ground and Erin gazed at her pale, smooth skin.

Erin stood and pulled the harness up over her hips. As she felt the straps between her legs, she felt the heat of her own desire for Alex, which was still so strong. The dildo was a shimmery gold silicone and thick, but specifically not in any way realistic. When searching online for the perfect strap-on, neither of them had wanted to imitate a penis. Erin took the dildo in her hand and slid it into place in the harness, then tightened the supple leather straps.

She moved across the room toward Alex, who was sitting on the edge of the wide window seat.

Alex waited for her, naked and smiling.

"So, Princess Alexandra," Erin said as she put

her right hand between Alex's breasts and pushed her willing body back on to the padded seat. "You must be excited if you want me to fuck you with this big gold dick." Erin's hands moved to Alex's inner thighs, which rose immediately in gooseflesh as she pulled them apart. Alex's breathing quickened.

Erin ran her hands down Alex's body, over her prominent collarbones, her full breasts, over her narrow ribcage and down over her stomach. Erin loved how every part of Alex's body reacted to her touch, her body almost shaking as Erin's hands moved over her.

"What would you like, Princess Alexandra?" Erin watched the glistening wetness between Alex's legs, but purposefully delayed touching her there.

She enjoyed teasing Alex like this. She enjoyed watching as cool confident Princess Alexandra was lost so deeply in lust for Erin that she was blushing and struggling to speak.

"Say the words, Lex."

"Please, fuck me. I need you inside me," Alex breathed.

"Just how badly do you need me?" Erin ran the fingers of her right hand down through

Alex's wetness as she asked. Alex's body jumped.

"Really fucking badly. Please. I am so turned on. Please. I need you."

Erin could feel how ready Alex was, and she positioned the golden dildo to Alex's slick folds. She teased a little with it, running it up and down Alex, pushing it against her clit and eliciting a deep moan. She used the fingers of her right hand to guide the head of it into Alex while her left hand free to hold Alex's hip steady. She moved her own body forward as the dildo slowly pushed deep inside Alex, causing her to gasp.

"You okay?" Erin whispered.

"Yes," Alex moaned, her hands reaching forward and grasping the straps on the leather harness to pull Erin all the way inside her until their bodies met. Alex's eyes were glazed.

Erin moved her right hand to Alex's left hip and held her body still while she began to slowly fuck her. She marvelled at the beauty of the light dancing across Alex below her and she loved how big her hands looked on Alex's body.

Alex moaned every time Erin pushed into her and her body relaxed into the dildo. Erin gave it to her as hard as she knew Alex craved. There was something about a hard fucking that took Alex away from the pressure of being Princess Alexandra and brought her right into the moment, where it was okay to just let go. Erin loved being able to give her that freedom. Sex for Alex was so much more than just sex.

Erin felt the pressure from the base of the dildo against her own clit as she thrust into Alex and her clit rose against it.

Erin moved her right hand and placed it palm down on Alex's pubic mound. The blonde hair was soft against her hand. Her thumb slid against Alex's clit as she continued to fuck her. She felt Alex's stomach muscles begin to tighten and she cried out, signifying the beginning of her orgasm, and she watched as Alex peaked and unravelled beneath her, her head rolling back. Her whole body rose in gooseflesh as her orgasm rippled through her. Erin watched for a minute, smiling to herself.

Erin pulled out and loosened the harness, stepping out of it.

"Lex, I'm so close, can you just lend me your mouth for a second?"

Alex's eyes opened and a smile washed over her face as she sat up, swaying slightly as she slid down off the seat onto her knees on the thick carpet. She moved straight between Erin's legs and her mouth sought out Erin's pleasure. Within seconds of feeling the heat of Alex's mouth on her, Erin ground into Alex's face and felt her own climax crash over her like a wave, running through every inch of her body. Erin's knees felt suddenly like jelly, so she collapsed to the floor with Alex and pulled her down onto the floor and into a deep kiss. She tasted her own orgasm on Alex's tongue, and the heat of desire ran through them both.

"You are perfect, Lex," she smiled. Alex was lying on top of her, and as usual, she felt small in her arms. Erin loved how Alex's body folded so perfectly into her own. She smelled Alex's shampoo strongly in her wet hair, tangling with the scent of their sex. That was the warm smell of home to Erin. Their connection was magical.

There was a loud knock on the door to their bedroom. Audrey suddenly woke from her slumber and gave a half-hearted bark from the four-poster bed. She had never been much of a guard dog. "Ma'am, Ms. Erin. It's just me."

Alicia, thought Erin. *Hair and makeup. Charity dinner. Shit.* They both snapped out of their blissful world. She felt Alex tense and become alert in her arms. Alex was instantly the princess again.

"Wait outside, please, Alicia." Alex was immediately commanding and powerful in her tone.

"Of course, Ma'am. Sorry to disturb."

Alex stood up and reached out to pull Erin up from the floor. "So, I think we both need a quick shower before we let Alicia in." She led Erin by the hand to the bathroom.

Erin smiled and allowed herself to be led by the enigmatic princess.

I will follow you anywhere, anytime.

2

Alex sat in front of the mirror as Alicia worked her magic with a hair dryer. Alex's trademark ash blonde bob was freshly highlighted and shimmering—almost silver in the light. She knew tonight was going to be a big night. It would be her first public appearance with Erin. Since Alex had come out publicly over four months ago, she had protected Erin in every way she could. She wanted to protect the sanctity of their relationship for as long as she could, without pushing Erin onto the world stage. She needed that kind of publicity to be entirely Erin's choice. Erin needed to decide that this was the life she wanted.

And she had done just that. Alex had kept her

in their bubble in the castle and it had felt almost magical. Of course, Alex had garnered so much more attention and questioning by the press after her recent revelations, whenever she had appeared publicly, while Erin had been shielded.

Erin had been briefed extensively about what it might be like to be the partner of someone like Princess Alexandra, but all the royal advisors could do was to educate Erin about what had happened historically and what they thought it might be like now. There would, of course, be extra pressure because of the whole *first lesbian princess* thing.

Alex had spoken at length with Erin, time and time again, in the privacy of their bedroom.

"Do you want this?"

"Are you sure you can handle this?"

"Are you sure you understand what you are signing up for?"

Erin had just nodded and said she was sure. That she wanted to be with Alex and that she would do whatever it took.

Alex still wasn't sure Erin really got it—that she really understood that she was sacrificing her freedom in order to be Alex's partner—but nevertheless, Alex wanted her to do it. So very badly.

She craved Erin with an intensity that scared

her. She longed for the sanctuary and protection that Erin offered her, and the freedom to be really and truly herself that she had found with Erin. She loved that Erin never judged. She just accepted and adored Alex in every way—and it wasn't because of who Princess Alexandra was. It was actually in spite of who she was.

Alex gazed over at Erin, who was ready and waiting for her, reclining on a chaise lounge and absorbed in her phone. Erin wore black fitted dress pants and a striking emerald green silk button-down shirt. The colour of the shirt brought out the dark green of her eyes. Her dark brown hair, which had always been slicked back into a bun when Erin had been a bodyguard, had been pinned up neatly by Alicia in a way that lifted her face and looked quite smart, professional, and powerful. The look had been paired with minimal makeup, and Erin looked stunning.

Alicia and Natalie—Alex's personal stylist and dresser—had taken Erin's androgynous style and had worked with it. Alex still melted into a puddle every time she looked across at her. Alex was happy that they hadn't tried to change the Erin that she had fallen in love with too much. Erin was still that delicious combination of masculine and feminine, and they hadn't shied away from that when styling her.

Alex smiled to herself. *That's my girlfriend. My actual girlfriend. I'm going out on a real date tonight. We are going out to appear at a function for my new LGBTQ charity, Rainbows.*

Alex was still in sweatpants. She would dress properly once her hair had been done. Alex would be wearing a long, emerald-green velvet sheath dress that would match perfectly with Erin's outfit. For once, Alex was excited to be photographed. She was genuinely excited for their first real photos together—aside from the couple selfies Alex had regularly taken from their life together, that obviously would never be shared. There were no public photos of Alex looking anything less than perfect.

Left to her own devices, Alex liked to make faces when taking selfies with Erin. She liked to cram Audrey's massive head between the two of their faces and to snap photos of the three of them. Erin would be laughing, Audrey would be drooling/ closing her eyes/ looking the other way—she was not a photogenic dog—and Alex would make a face. She would make any face that wasn't

Princess Alexandra's wide and instantly recognisable smile.

These were her favourite photos. Of her little family, just the three of them.

Still, Alex was excited to see the photos from tonight. She wanted to see Princess Alexandra partnered by her gorgeous girlfriend as much as the rest of the world did. She wanted to see her small frame leaning into Sergeant Erin Kennedy in a way that, so far, she had only done privately. She wanted the world to see how in love she was.

There was a knock on the door to their private quarters. Erin looked up and then to Alex.

Alex still led things. She was still the princess. "Come in," she called loudly.

The door swung open and in came Alex's new bodyguard, Joanne. "Ma'am, can I have two minutes with yourself and Sergeant Kennedy, please?"

"I'm finished, Ma'am. I'll leave you." Alicia smiled, while adding a final spritz of hairspray to Alex's ice-blonde hair. Alex smiled; she looked good. "Perfect. Thank you, Alicia." Alex stood and gestured for Joanne and Erin to come toward the seating area.

Alex was still trying to get used to Joanne—

Sergeant Joanne Davis. Before Erin, she had always hated when her security detail changed. Alex liked to feel safe. She liked to trust someone, and needed her bodyguard to know her and understand her needs and wants. Unfortunately. that only came with time. She had enjoyed that feeling of security with Erin. Their connection had been natural and instinctual, perhaps hastened by the lust she had quickly come to feel for Erin.

Sergeant Davis was different. She was older than Alex, maybe fifteen years so. She was intensely private and very serious. She seemed very guarded, but then Alex wasn't too surprised by that. She imagined that Joanne had been briefed that Princess Alexandra liked to fuck her bodyguards, and that Joanne was to stay completely professional at all times.

Alex didn't, as it happened, like to fuck her bodyguards. Over the years, there had been various bodyguards. There had been many different staff members and friends, and Alex had been attracted to different women over the years. She had even thought she was in love once, but nobody had affected her like Erin had.

Alex had never contemplated coming out before, and although she was glad she had now, she knew that she never would have come out without the intensity of feeling that had overwhelmed her. Without what she felt for Erin. Alex knew for sure that she would have married a very suitable man—as she was expected to—and birthed the children that she was also expected to. She would have buried her truth so very deeply and kept it buried for many years, perhaps even for the rest of her life. Alex knew she would have continued to cry late at night in the dark, when she was alone. Cry for the loss of the life she had been too scared to choose. And she knew that she wouldn't have been the first woman to do so.

But Erin had given Alex the strength to live her truth. There was something about the magical ease she experienced with Erin, which felt meant to be. It had been different before, with the other women she had desired. She might have craved them physically, but she had never been able to find that emotional closeness that allowed her to be herself. And learning to truly be herself, Alex realized, was the only way she could really give herself over physically.

Alex had never imagined that she could be as sexually free as she had with Erin. Erin had unleashed a hunger within her that had been there for so many years. And before that, Alex had been unaware of it. But now she couldn't get enough of the lean musculature of Erin's body. She couldn't get enough of discovering new things sexually. Alex wanted to try everything with Erin, to make up for the many years when she had tried nothing.

Alex sat next to Erin and leaned into her, kissing her neck. She inhaled deeply, smelling the spicy heat of the unisex perfume she had bought for Erin—*Fucking Fabulous by Tom Ford*. Alex had always loved the scent of it, as well as its sleek black bottle. She always smiled to herself at the name. The intense fragrance suited Erin perfectly. Erin's arm snaked around Alex's back and settled on her left thigh. *God, she looks so gorgeous*, Alex thought. *I wish she could take me now.*

"Ma'am, Sergeant Kennedy . . . " Joanne looked between the two of them slightly awkwardly, which snapped Alex back into the present.

Start behaving like a princess and not a dumb lovestruck teenager, Alex.

Alex sat up straight and ignored the burning heat of Erin's strong fingers on her thigh.

"Sergeant Davis. Of course. Please speak."

Joanne smiled and continued, directing her

speech mainly to Alex, "Ma'am, you should be aware that there are some right-wing activists planning to protest against homosexuality at your charity event this evening. While there has been a huge amount of support in so many places for your coming out, as I am sure you are aware, there has also been hate. People who have a political agenda to discredit the crown are jumping on the lesbian thing. They are using it as an opportunity to discredit you. There are also questions about the young people who could be affected by the work of Rainbows."

"Supporting LGBTQ youth is a crime now?" Alex asked. Erin squeezed her hand.

"Not at all, Ma'am. But I'm sure you know that there are people who don't think that LGBTQ education should be allowed in schools. I know this a big thing your charity is working on."

"I think education of youth is vital for a wider understanding and acceptance of LGBTQ identities in the future, and I will not back down on that, Sergeant Davis. What are you suggesting?"

"Nothing major yet, Ma'am. I just wanted to keep you abreast of the situation, as you have asked. This evening, we can expect homophobic protestors outside the function. We don't think it will be a good time to pose for photos as a lesbian couple outside the venue. We were hoping you would agree to being swept inside quickly."

"That, I won't, Sergeant Davis. Sergeant Kennedy and I will stand for photos for the press, and autographs as arranged, for thirty minutes before we go into the event. I am not ashamed of my sexuality, nor am I ashamed of my charity's work. I will not back down. You and the security team will watch the protestors. Erin and I will be the positive representation that this world needs. I will not back down."

"I thought you might say that, Ma'am. Thank you for your time. I will ensure that we manage the protestors. I will see you at the car shortly." Joanne nodded and stepped out of the room, closing the door softly.

Alex sighed wearily. "It won't be easy." She shook her head.

Erin took Alex's face in her hands and turned it to her. "Hey, Lex, look at me. We knew this wouldn't be easy. But you are right, we won't back down. We expected a fight and we are here for it. I've got you. I'm at your side. I'll never let them hurt you. You are right; we will be the lesbian couple the world needs to see. I've got you." She leaned in and kissed Alex deeply, and desire slid straight through Alex's body. She broke the kiss. She knew this wasn't the time, but she snuggled herself into Erin's arms, losing herself in Erin's chest.

She needed a minute. Just a minute to melt into her protector and feel like the weight of the world wasn't on her shoulders. She nuzzled into Erin, who stroked her hair tenderly. Erin seemed to instinctively know what she needed—when she needed to feel safe in Erin's strong arms.

Alex took a deep breath. "Okay, I'm ready."

3

Erin was dazzled by flashbulbs outside the hotel as she got out of the black Range Rover. They had arrived for the Rainbows dinner. Erin wasn't used to having car doors opened for her. It felt familiar to be at Alex's side—but as her shadow, rather than her partner.

Things were very different now.

She looked at Alex for a second. Her hair shimmered an icy silver in the light, while the green velvet clung perfectly to her body. Alex's bright blue eyes lit up as she smiled widely for the press. She was exquisite. She was the princess the nation loved, and she was Erin's.

Erin still couldn't believe it. Alex leaned into her and held her hand, whispering to her, "Smile!"

Erin tried to do the bold smile Alex had made her practice at home. At first, it felt so alien and unnatural. People were calling loudly to them from behind the press barrier. "Princess! Alexandra! Sergeant Kennedy! Over here!" Erin held tightly to Alex's hand and let her lead. She fixed the smile on her face and looked from camera to camera, standing tall and proud as Alex did all the posing. She was, as ever, a natural. She held Erin's hand, pulled her close, leaned into her, and made her laugh. Everything looked so natural when Alex did it, even the way she moved her body against and next to Erin's, giving the press different angles and shots to be photographed.

Erin had looked in the mirror before they left and couldn't believe what she saw. She didn't look like herself. She looked like someone so glamorous. The emerald silk was beautiful and had been cut to fit her wide shoulders and muscled arms. Erin had always hated shopping, so she had to admit that this was one of the perks to being with Alex. Natalie, who worked for Alex as a dresser and stylist, was now styling Erin too. She had measured Erin from top to toe and then had left, only to return with a wardrobe full of beautiful clothes for Erin to wear, for every occasion.

Erin had worried they would try and put her in feminine dresses, to make her into something she wasn't, so she was so grateful that they hadn't. Every single thing Natalie had made her try on had looked great, and Erin had felt comfortable and not compromised in any way.

Whether she was working or not, Erin had always liked to dress in a way that would allow her to run and fight if she had to. She had said this to Natalie right up front, and Natalie had laughed as if she had made a joke. Her eyes had sparkled and she said she would do the best she could.

And she had. Erin loved the choice of flat leather brogues and wingtips Natalie had filled her wardrobe with. Every shoe had been exquisitely made. As Erin tested the feel of them, she knew she would be able to run in them if she needed to. That made her happy.

Erin and Alex had started signing autographs for a selection of LGBTQ youth who had been invited to the dinner. They were doing it outside the hotel to allow the press to get their photos—and to allow the world media to see them together for the first time.

Erin couldn't stop her eyes from straying to the right of the hotel entrance, where the anti-LGBT protesters were. They held placards. They shouted obscenities at Erin and at the princess. Although she was no longer Alex's bodyguard, Erin found herself instinctively positioning her body between Alex and the threat, to offer protection. She wasn't sure she would ever be able to stop protecting Alex, whether it was her job or not.

Erin felt so fiercely protective of her girlfriend, now even more so. So she angled her body as she would, had she been working, and she remained alert. Erin knew damn well that arriving or leaving known public locations would be the riskiest times for a public figure like Princess Alexandra.

Alex was working, too. Her voice was warm and friendly to the young people. Her smile was genuine now; Erin could tell the difference. This was Alex's passion. She didn't want anyone to have to grow up in the closet, as she had. She wanted wider acceptance, visibility, and inclusivity. She wanted to be a powerful force for change, and Erin didn't doubt her for a second.

Though diminutive in appearance, Princess Alexandra was a force of nature. Erin smiled. She loved seeing Alex like this. While she couldn't let go of her awareness of the threat, Erin split herself between scouting for danger and smiling and talking to the young people. Not to mention signing autographs.

Sergeant Erin Kennedy. She signed her name and rank. Not that Erin really had a rank or even a job anymore,. Still, the Met Police continued to employ her, purely to use her for good publicity. They had said something about a teaching role, but nothing had materialized. Erin had become convinced that they just wanted to keep her on so they could ride off the back of her new-found fame. The association of the police force with the darling of the royal family, who just so happened to also be a lesbian, was PR gold for the Metropolitan Police. It made them look inclusive and it made them look good. And the royal family media team liked that she was a Sergeant as well. It was a title of sorts, and they liked how it looked next to Princess Alexandra's name.

Erin glanced around for a minute at the craziness of the press, the protesters, and the teenagers who were clamouring for attention from the couple.

This is my life now. It will be like this everywhere we go. Am I ready for this? she thought.

The dinner had been beautiful, with Erin treated like royalty. She was used to disappearing somewhere to wait, while Alex attended dinners like this. Occasionally, staff would be brought trays of snacks, but often Erin would remain hungry till she made it home, late in the evening. How times had changed. Alex had taught her at home how to use cutlery—it was complicated when there were multiple forks, knives, and courses to deal with. There had been more training than Erin had imagined so she could take on the role of Alex's girlfriend, but she had taken it on and had never questioned anything. She always wanted to make Alex proud and never to let her down. Knowing the customs of the upper classes—how people behaved within royal circles—was a huge part of that.

Erin had to learn how to be in Alex's world. She had also been taking lessons in how to speak properly from the royal family's media department, as well as instruction about how to answer questions in public. They hadn't been very impressed when words like *fuck* accidentally slipped into conversation. But Erin had a lot more control now. She thought carefully before she spoke. Each word was selected carefully and she rarely stuttered anymore when she felt awkward. She just took a deep breath, calmed herself, counted to three in her head, and then said what she wanted to say.

Being able to sit at Alex's side at the top of the table and see how she made the whole table fall in love with her made Erin happy.

God, she is incredible.

They started to say their goodbyes, with Erin taking Alex's lead. Her jacket was brought to her and she was helped on with it. As they exited the big hall, Joanne fell into step just behind Alex, quite close. Erin knew there was a reason for that. Joanne's eyes met Erin's and Erin nodded imperceptibly to say she understood, and closed in on the other side of Alex.

She knew Alex understood what their proximity meant as well, but Alex continued to smile, say goodbyes, and be dazzling. She didn't react. Erin was in full high-alert mode now; she might not officially be Alex's bodyguard and they would no longer let her carry a gun, but she damn well was ready for anything. The doors opened and the noise started. The protesters were loudly chanting, "Being gay is a sin! No Lesbian Queen!" Erin caught sight of a big sign that read, *The Church Condemns Homosexuality*.

Alex remained unfazed.

Erin saw the black Range Rover just outside the steps. Another member of the security team stood by the door to the back seat, ready to open it for them.

Alex, Erin and Joanne exited the doors, with Erin and Joanne flanking Alex closely on either side. The protesters had quadrupled in number from earlier. Suddenly they closed in, bursting through the barriers in an angry mob.

Erin and Joanne acted in a split second—each grabbing one of Alex's arms and sprinting toward the Range Rover with her. Erin bundled the princess quickly into the back seat and jumped in next to her.

The Range Rover sped off immediately. Erin saw Joanne jump into the back-up vehicle and it lined up close behind them. Erin felt her heart racing.

"Are you okay?" She looked to Alex. "Did we hurt you? I'm sorry; we just needed to move you fast. We couldn't let those people get close to you. Who knows what they would have done?"

Alex's eyes were wide and she looked as flustered as Alex ever got.

"Thank you," she said. "I know you aren't officially my protector anymore, but it always reassures me when you are there. I trust you. You thought there was a threat, so I will excuse you for the bruises you two have no doubt left on my arms!"

"Oh god, Alex, I'm sorry."

Alex put her hand on Erin's thigh. "I'm just teasing. Thank you for protecting me. I will always be grateful to you. I know Rainbows makes us a target and I know that stresses you out. I am sorry for that. But what we are doing is so important—you know that, don't you? Visibility is everything. We can change the world, you know. I really believe that."

Erin smiled wryly, calmer now that the Range Rover was driving safely through the darkness, and no sign of threat anymore.

"God, you are a challenge, Princess Alexandra. Keeping you safe is my absolute priority. Still, you know I will support you one hundred percent, in anything you choose to do. You are incredible. Your speech tonight was amazing and you are an absolute inspiration. Seeing those teenage girls and boys looking up to you was so cool. You are 'being that change' in the world already. I'm so very proud of you and everything you do, you know."

Alex's eyes glowed and she smiled. "I'm so lucky. I love you so much, Erin. What do you think Audrey is doing?"

"I bet she is stretched out right across the middle of our bed drooling on it. And I also bet she doesn't move when we get in."

Alex laughed. "I mean she has the biggest and *most* luxurious dog bed money can buy, yet she still chooses ours whenever she thinks she can get away with it."

"That's because our bed is the *actual* biggest and most luxurious bed money can buy. I didn't even know they made beds that big." Erin poked Alex in the ribs and she yelped.

"Well, that's a good thing because now I have to share it with you and Audrey, and neither of you are small!" Alex laughed and took Erin's arm and snuggled in underneath it. "God, I'm tired, I can't wait to get home."

Audrey resisted being evicted from their bed by playing dead. Eventually Erin lured her with a treat into her own big bed, and as Audrey would do anything for food it worked well. Erin kissed the top of the dog's head. "G'night, big girl."

She wandered back over to the bed in only her underwear and watched as Alex took her jewelry off. "You know, it's so good that we can get one of the staff to mind Audrey when we are gone for hours like that. I know she isn't really that concerned when we leave, but it would make me sad to think that she was on her own for ages, or like she wanted to go outside and there was no one to take her."

"One of the many perks to being royalty," Alex smiled. "No shortage of people to do everything for you. You know, there was a queen called Queen Anne, in 1702. She ruled from her bed and had everything brought to her there, including her meetings with the Prime Minister and the politicians. I *love* that. Maybe I will be a queen like that. Just lying in my bed demanding shit be done for me!" She laughed as she slipped the green dress down off her shoulders. It dropped like liquid, straight to the floor. Erin couldn't stop her eyes from jumping to Alex's body, which was only covered in a tiny, white lace thong.

"Oh, you'll be a queen who spends most of her time on her back in bed, will you?" Erin grabbed Alex and lifted her off the ground, swinging her up into her arms. Alex screamed and laughed as Erin turned and threw her on her back onto the bed. Alex was giggling. She was so very beautiful without her makeup and jewelry. Erin jumped on top of her and pinned her, tickling her. Alex giggled some more. Erin's right thigh was firmly wedged between Alex's legs and Erin watched as the giggles slowed and lust glazed Alex's eyes.

"What's up, Princess Alexandra? Did you want something?"

Alex nodded. "Mm hm. I want your mouth all over my body."

"And people usually do what you say, don't they?" Erin pressed her right thigh tighter into Alex and felt hot, wet heat against it.

"Yes, they do." Alex nodded earnestly. "I am a princess, after all."

Erin knelt back up and peeled Alex's thong down off her hips and right down her legs, throwing it to the corner of the room. There was nothing she enjoyed more than feasting on Alex's body. She lay on top of Alex, pinning her wrists down to the bed. "Stay still," Erin whispered as she kissed Alex's mouth, her face, her ear. Erin ran her tongue around Alex's ear, sucking her earlobe into her mouth and pushing her tongue into Alex's ear. She felt Alex moaning underneath her. "I'm going to kiss every inch of your body and make you come in my mouth," she whispered, then went began to suck on Alex's earlobe again. She kissed her neck and collarbones. Alex melted beneath her. Erin knew she was driving Alex crazy. Her mouth was soon on Alex's breast. She kissed and sucked on Alex's nipple and heard her moaning. She felt goosebumps running across her smooth skin.

Erin sucked hard and Alex yelped, but she knew Alex enjoyed that. She felt Alex mashing her pussy tighter against Erin's hipbone as she nibbled and sucked Alex's erect nipples. Erin loved how turned on and excited Alex got. Like sex was always a novelty, something that she had missed out on for so many years.

She ran her tongue down over Alex's ribs and noticed that they weren't quite as prominent as they had been. Erin was happy about that. She didn't like that Alex felt so much pressure from the world to be so very thin. She wanted Alex to settle in a weight that was natural for her, and not created under pressure she felt from a fucked up world. Erin just wanted to love her however she was. She kissed Alex's side and her belly and Alex giggled again. Her laughter was music to Erin; she was obsessed with it. She loved making Alex laugh like that.

Erin's hungry mouth moved to Alex's groin and she settled between Alex's legs, kissing lightly down over her sex and her inner thighs. She teased her, her tongue running lightly down the crease of Alex's pussy. Her mouth took one of Alex's labia lightly inside and sucked it. Every time she casually brushed Alex's clit in passing, she felt her body leap. Alex was moaning and writhing beneath her. "Please, please. I need you."

Alex's begging was the sweetest sound, and Erin pushed her tongue inside Alex as far as she could. She licked in long strokes, up and down. She pushed Alex's legs up and over her shoulders and tongued from Alex's asshole right up through her wetness to her clit. She felt Alex's body begin to tighten as she got closer and closer, and Erin pushed her fingers suddenly and deeply inside

Alex as her tongue moved its firm strokes up to Alex's clit. Her fingers curled upwards and began to fuck Alex, while her tongue was insistent on Alex's clit. Alex gripped a handful of Erin's hair tightly as she tensed and orgasmed loudly, crying out as she came.

Her wetness gushed over Erin's mouth and hand. As usual, making Alex come was one of the most satisfying things ever.

Alex lay back and giggled in satisfaction. "God, that was so good!" she said. "You are such an expert!"

Erin laughed and lay on top of her again, feeling the sweat on their naked skin mingling between them.

Alex pushed Erin off her suddenly. "I want to make you come," she said brightly like a child with a plan. Erin lay back on the bed and smiled. "Oh, do you now?"

"Yes. Have I got permission to do whatever I like?" Alex had a naughty look in her eye.

Erin laughed. "Oh, sure. Go on then." Their sex life had been like this. Alex was determined to try absolutely everything there was, and Erin enjoyed experiencing everything with her. Even though she had tried so much before, it was different with Alex. It always was. Her enthusiasm was infectious and boundless.

Alex pulled out some silk ties from her bedside drawer and bound each of Erin's wrists to the posts at the head of the bed. She repeated the process with Erin's ankles , tying them to the posts at the foot of the bed—after she had pulled Erin's underwear off over her hips.

"So, I ordered something new." Alex smiled and brandished a glass dildo that she had pulled from her bedside drawer. It was exquisitely crafted, beautiful and obviously expensive. The glass was long and slim and had beautiful smooth ripples along its length. "I know how you like the steel dildos we have, so I was thinking we could see what glass feels like. Something else that is beautiful, cold, hard, and hopefully amazing." Alex's eyes were bright. The bedside light cast a golden glow over Alex and the toy. Erin smiled.

"Whatever you want, Princess Alexandra. I can't exactly resist now, can I?" Erin teasingly and halfheartedly fought against her bindings. She knew if she really wanted to free herself, she could.

Alex placed the dildo on the bed between

Erin's legs along with a bottle of lube. She lay alongside Erin with her mouth at Erin's breast and took Erin's right nipple in her mouth and began to suck.

Oh God, she knows that drives me crazy.

Erin couldn't take her eyes off Alex's face and how beautiful her mouth looked suckling on Erin. Her nipple felt like it should always be in Alex's mouth. Meanwhile Alex's right hand delved between her legs, sliding easily through hot, wet folds. She slid her hand up and down teasingly and without intent. It was driving Erin crazy. She wanted to come so badly. She was so turned on from fucking Alex. She felt her hips rising involuntarily to meet Alex's hand, trying to seek out the pressure she so desperately craved.

The next thing Erin felt was cold lube as it hit her clit and then Alex's hot hand as she spread it around. Across her pussy and down onto her asshole. She felt Alex's delicate fingers running round the rim of her ass, slick with lube and then one of her fingers pushing gently inside. It felt exquisite and electric. Erin felt no pain, only pleasure, and at no point did Alex stop sucking her nipple.

Erin relaxed and let Alex play with her ass. It

was relatively new to her, but she always let Alex explore her body in any way she wanted. She had found herself with Alex, finding pleasure in so many new things.

She felt Alex's slippery fingers probing her, feeling her deep inside. Then suddenly she felt the cold hard touch of the glass dildo at her asshole as Alex's mouth was still busy on her nipple. She felt relaxed for it and not worried as it pushed gently into her. Bigger than Alex's slim fingers, but not uncomfortably so. Erin felt electricity rush right through her body as Alex fucked her gently with the glass dildo that soon enough felt hot inside of her. Very hot. Erin opened her eyes and saw Alex's beautiful lips closed around her nipple and her eyelashes flickering as she worked.

God, she is so beautiful.

Erin couldn't hold back any longer and orgasmed hard and without warning. There was an intensity and rush to her orgasm from anal that nothing else really compared to. Erin rode the wave of it, tensed against her restraints, and then she relaxed and smiled. "Fuck yes. Okay, I love that new toy."

Alex smiled as she cleaned up, taking the dildo to the bathroom and untying the silk ties.

She got back into bed and Erin got under the covers with her. They tangled up in each other's arms. Erin felt Alex nuzzle into her and felt her breathing slow and regulate as she fell asleep. Erin fell asleep then, breathing her in.

4

The next morning, Alex requested the morning newspapers be brought to her. She browsed through the photos of herself and Erin from the night before as she sat on their small balcony, enjoying her coffee in her robe in the weak sunshine. Audrey had been taken out for a brief walk by one of the staff, and now she lay content at Alex's feet as Alex flicked through the newspapers. She wasn't surprised to see herself and Alex on the front page of every newspaper.

They looked as incredible together as she had hoped they would. Erin was so tall, strong, and handsome while Alex looked delicate, blonde, and beautiful next to her. The matching of her dress with Erin's shirt had been noted. Their connection was obvious to anyone. Erin's hand on her hip. Alex's face smiling up at Erin's. Alex whispering in her ear. The photos were perfect. The reporting was mostly positive, but highlighted the presence of the protesters and the fact that Alex was rushed away after the event. A couple of the reports had focused on Alex's charity and its potentially harmful ideas that children in schools should be exposed to homosexuality.

Alex sighed. She had known it wouldn't be easy, but she also knew that it was important that the existence of LGBTQ people was taught in schools. She knew it was important that children had an awareness that many different family set-ups existed, and that not every family had a mummy, a daddy, and two children.

She had plans to ride out with Erin this morning and then a meeting with her father, the king, afterward. She wasn't sure what he was going to bring up this time. They would probably review Rainbows and its proposed work, her relationship with Erin and how it was going, and what was next.

Erin appeared next to her on the balcony in a tight tank top that showed off the her arm muscles. Her hair was messy and her face still creased with sleep. Alex thought how very lovely she looked in the morning light.

Alex smiled at her. "Good Morning, beautiful. Welcome to fame." She nodded to the newspapers and Erin smiled lazily in response as she looked at the photos of them together.

I'm so lucky, Alex thought to herself.

It was a sunny winter morning and the horses were fresh and excited to be out. Alex rode Sebastian, her favourite horse. He was a small, compact bay horse. Erin had taken a liking to Amber, a feisty chestnut mare that Alex had never really formed a connection with. Amber wasn't an easy ride and that was probably why Alex had avoided her. She was surprised, in fact, that the palace had kept Amber. It was well known that they wouldn't let Alex ride the difficult horses, even if she had wanted to. The princess was too precious and needed to be kept safe, and not to be put at risk of injury. But Erin always seemed to enjoy the spirited horses . She was such a skilled and confident rider that Alex enjoyed watching the two of them together.

"How are you feeling after last night?" Erin asked, as they walked the horses through the private estate woodland together.

"After the sex or the protesters?" Alex looked at her.

Erin laughed. "Well, I was meaning after the protesters, but, you know, whatever you want to give me!"

"Well, firstly, the sex was incredible. I slept *so* well. Secondly, I'm not worried. That's why I have a security team. The plan will go on. I'm meeting my father later today, so I will need to explain everything to him. Rainbows is doing good work though. You can see it already, can't you? It was so nice to meet those teenagers yesterday. Our visibility as a couple, too, is huge. We are by far the most high-profile lesbian couple in the world.... How are you feeling about that?"

"Um, well, you are right, the publicity is bigger than I had ever imagined. But I can do it; I'm sure. It's just getting used to having my photo taken, right?" Erin suddenly reminded Alex of the awkward bodyguard she had been when Alex had first met her.

"Oh, just that and being a role model for queer youth all over the world!" Alex said boldly.

Erin laughed, "So no pressure or anything?"

"No pressure at all, but just don't fuck it up." Alex smirked.

"*Oh my god,* <u>as</u> <u>if</u> you just said *fuck*! Princess Alexandra doesn't say *fuck*."

"She's learned bad language from screwing her hot bodyguard."

They both laughed.

"Come on," Alex said. "Let's go for a canter and do some jumps. Just the little ones. I promise I won't fall off and get injured. Okay?"

"You know you aren't supposed to, right? You're not to take unnecessary risks." Erin looked at her, serious for a minute. Alex was a good rider and the risk was minimal, but when jumping horses, the risk was always there.

"You aren't part of my security team anymore, Sergeant Kennedy. I think you should chill out and leave Joanne to start stressing when we canter off." Alex squeezed her horse forward and Amber was quick to follow into a canter.

"You are getting *so* naughty lately, Princess Alexandra!" Erin called from behind Alex.

"I mean you could spank me for it, but you would have to catch me first, Sergeant Kennedy!" Alex called back into the wind.

Alex felt alive and in the moment—a presence of mind she was finding she needed more now that she was with Erin. Being with Erin gave her tastes of freedom and she loved every second of that. Galloping around the estate and through the trees was fun. She turned her horse toward one of the jumps, a felled tree trunk. Sebastian never thought twice, taking it in his stride and clearing the log. Alex smiled. This was great! She could hear Amber thundering along behind her. She turned and took on another fence, wooden rails this time. She checked Sebastian's speed slightly and he responded. He really was a lovely horse. He slowed his pace slightly and cleared the rails easily.

Alex smiled as she steered between more and more of the jumps, enjoying herself and building her confidence after each one under her belt. It had been years since she had done anything like this. Her security team was probably having a breakdown, but Alex didn't care. She needed this in her life; she realized. And on a horse as beautifully trained and careful as Sebastian, where was the risk?

Alex steered him through the trees, with the dappled sunlight bathing her face in warmth, and smiled to herself. She was so happy she could burst.

"Alexandra," her father nodded to her as she entered his office. "Please sit."

Alex immediately noticed that her father's head of security was also in the meeting. He was a tall, quiet man named Rob Greene. Alex remembered that.

She pulled up the chair opposite King George's big desk and took a seat. The king looked tired. Older perhaps, she thought, as she studied his face. Would the stress of ruling the country age her as it had him?

"Now, I won't beat around the bush here. Rob is here because of the current threats to your security, of which I'm sure you are aware. Rob, please speak freely to Alexandra."

Alex looked at Rob. "Ma'am. I'm sure you know that there are people in this country who do not want a queen who doesn't fit their ideals of what a queen should be. Your *alternative* choice of lifestyle doesn't sit well with them. We believe they are being pushed and incited by powerful people with certain political agendas. They feel threatened by your power and the love the people of this country have for you. We have reviewed your popularity among the people since your announcement over the summer, and the majority of the population of this kingdom still love you. You have been the queen of their hearts for so long, their golden girl, that as we predicted, they are supporting you through this. We are only talking about a very small group who don't, but unfortunately, we think they are being pushed and funded by someone else."

"Whom?" Alex asked, curious.

"We don't know for sure yet. We are investigating. But it has to be someone connected to the extreme right political parties."

"What is the risk to me? I want you to speak openly to me. Do not for one second think I cannot take the truth, and do not treat me any differently because I am a woman."

"We think their agenda is to take you out. Without you, when the king dies, his younger brother, Prince Arthur would ascend to the throne. We are unsure if he has been compromised."

"By *take me out*, you mean I am a target for assassination?" Alex remained serious. Nothing was more serious. The words shocked her, but she couldn't afford to be scared. She knew that her position did not come without risk.

"Yes. We believe so." Rob was direct with her and she appreciated that, at least.

"Father, have you spoken to Uncle Arthur?" Alex looked at the king, questioningly.

"I obviously cannot ask him about this. But I have never trusted him. Arthur has always been a snake and he has hated being the *royal spare*. I am sorry to tell you that I believe he has always been jealous of me. I can also tell you that he is a misogynist—he never liked that I had one daughter and no sons. He never thought a girl would be worthy of the throne. It wouldn't surprise me, Alex, if your coming out has pushed him over the edge. A female heir to the throne is one thing. A female heir in a relationship with a woman may be one step too far for Arthur."

King George cleared his throat. "Alexandra, I know your decision over the summer came as a shock to me, but only because it was unexpected. I want you to know that I support you entirely. You are every bit my daughter. You have dedicated your life to what is best for this country and for the monarchy. This country could not have a better heir to the throne. What you are doing is your truth and I respect that wholeheartedly. Your truth is something the nation can get behind, and in living your truth, you will become nothing but stronger."

Alex smiled tightly. "Thank you, Father. Your support means a lot." She looked at Rob. "What is your advice to me? I will not back down. I will not hide."

"I know you won't, Princess Alexandra. The king and I have spoken, and we do not expect you to. Instead, we will tighten your security. We will increase the size of the team dedicated to you. We thought you would want to know."

"Thank you. Absolutely, I always want to know." She nodded to Rob.

"Rob, you are dismissed," the king's deep voice boomed. Rob nodded his respect and left the room like an obedient dog.

As the door closed, he looked to Alex, "Tell me, Alexandra. How is your relationship with Sergeant Kennedy? I have left you two to have your time together to get to know each other, and for you to make your own decisions."

Alex thought about Erin. "I love her, Father."

"You see a future with her?" He looked at her curiously.

"I do. Absolutely." Alex knew there was nothing she wanted more.

"What does that look like? Do you see marriage with Sergeant Kennedy?" Alex had expected this question and she knew it was complicated. The reigning monarch, her father, was the head of the Church of England—and the Church of England did not support same-sex marriage.

"It is something I would like, yes. But I realise the dilemma there." Alex knew she had to tread carefully. She appreciated her father's support and he had gone far beyond what she had expected so far.

"Dilemma?" He guffawed loudly. "More like a constitutional crisis. Whether we agree with it or we don't, the monarchy is archaic and I don't see the Church getting on board with a gay wedding—although I know there has been a huge amount of supposition in the media lately about what we are going to do."

He paused and picked up a mug of what Alex was fairly sure was whisky. The king thought that having it in a mug meant that nobody would realize what it was. He had always naively thought that.

Her father coughed loudly. "Alexandra, I believe that you should marry. I always have thought that. I also believe you should marry for love. You know your mother and I married for different reasons, and we have both regretted that for many years. But how we figure out your marriage one day will be another thing entirely. I can obviously influence the Church from my position, but I am not sure how wise that would be. There may be other options. Would the Church's approval be important to you?"

"Only because I have known my whole life that one day I will be expected to be the head of the Church of England when I am queen. I fear that perhaps my succession may be complicated by my marriage to a woman."

"Alexandra, I will speak to my advisors. It may be that the monarchy's partnership with the Church is no longer something that would be in the best interests of the country. It may be that you, the future of the monarchy, will change things—many things. I don't have the answers yet. But I do promise you a wedding, if that is what you decide you want. I realise it is still early days." He sighed loudly. Alex contemplated his words.

"Can we talk about children?"

"Of course, Father." Alex had thought about marriage and children a lot, but she had not yet brought either subject up with Erin. She knew Erin was adapting to so much already. She didn't want to push Erin too far or make her feel pressured. Being the girlfriend of Princess Alexandra was plenty of pressure for her to handle at the moment.

"Well, you know that there is still the hope and expectation that you will produce an heir. But we both know the child would need to be of your blood and born of you. I have organized an appointment for you with the top fertility expert in the country. Will you attend?"

"Happily, Father. Children are something that I want and it is still entirely possible." So many possibilities ran through Alex's head. "What are your thoughts on potential sperm donors?"

"I think we either need to go high profile, or else entirely anonymous. If the sperm were sourced anonymously, there would always be the risk of the donor coming to us in the future. For example, the child might look sufficiently like the donor—enough to be recognised—and then the donor could come to us with a claim. It wouldn't be such a bad idea to have someone high profile in mind instead. Legal agreements would be drawn up. I can have my people research and draw up a list of suitable candidates if you would like . . . " Her father looked at Alex intently.

Alex felt she finally had his respect. She felt like they were on the same team and he was treating her like an adult for once, and she liked it.

"We can hold onto that idea for now, okay? I will also think about possible candidates, and then we could meet and review them."

"Excellent plan, Alexandra. I would also like to plan a formal dinner for you and Sergeant Kennedy to attend, so that we can get to know her. I would like to meet her parents, too."

"Yes, Father. Please send me the details. Is that everything?"

He nodded to her and finished the liquid in his mug before leaning back in his chair. "It is."

She knew she was dismissed, so she nodded and headed out of the room.

5

Erin walked the grounds of the castle with Audrey, as she did every day. It was still winter, but spring was coming and the cool sunny day promised more to come. Audrey's big, gangly stride as she ran across the grass always amused Erin. Audrey was huge now. Her body hadn't quite filled out to go with her long, strong legs, but it soon would. Her fawn colouring shimmered in the sunlight.

Weeks had passed since Erin's first public outing with Alex, but they had appeared regularly in public as a couple. Every time, there were so many fans that it was overwhelming. Unfortunately, there were also protestors every time, with signs saying, *Homosexuality is a Sin* and *Say NO to a*

Lesbian Queen. This troubled Erin, but Alex refused to speak about it. Alex was adamant that they would continue forward and that they wouldn't be threatened by these people.

Now that Alex was back into her charity work and princess commitments, Erin was beginning to realize that life as a royal girlfriend was pretty lonely. Alex was a busy woman, and Erin was no longer needed to accompany her everywhere. She was no longer her bodyguard.

Erin needed her own life and interests, but soon realized that she had none. She had limited her own life for so long in order to focus on work —to learn to be the best bodyguard she could be. Being a bodyguard meant giving up your own life to be a shadow for someone else. But now that she was no longer needed as a shadow for Princess Alexandra, Erin needed something else. She needed a sense of purpose, but she was limited regarding what that could be.

Now that she had become known to the world as Princess Alexandra's girlfriend, the press were absolutely desperate to know more. There had been so many requests for interviews with Erin. She had even seen that old friends and family members had sold their stories about her to the press. Luckily, Erin had no major skeletons. A few ex-girlfriends, sure. But her family was terribly boring and there was nothing there that could be potentially damaging to Alex. The PR department for the royal family had investigated her history, her ex-girlfriends, and the members of Erin's family. They had dug up everything there was to dig up. Luckily Erin and the people who had been close to her were clean enough.

So now Erin was limited when it came to where she could go and what she could do, without being mobbed. The palace had offered to send security out with her, but she hated the idea of it. During her career as a bodyguard, Erin had always said that she never envied the client. That she would never trade with them. She had always said that having all the money and the fame in the world wasn't really worth it if you had no privacy. If you had to have a bodyguard go everywhere with you. Yet, here she was. She had traded places. All because of love. All because of Alex.

Alex. Whenever Erin thought about her, she was overwhelmed with love, lust, and the desire to care for and protect her. But she also knew that recently, Alex had been lying to her.

There was something that Alex was keeping

from Erin. It had started after Alex had met with her father. She had come home from that meeting and had been different. Alex hadn't said what the meeting was about and Erin hadn't felt it was her place to ask. Alex had carried on as normal, and she was a gifted actress. Erin knew Alex was good at hiding things. Her act would probably have fooled everyone else, but Erin saw through it. Erin saw the secret flash within Alex's blue eyes late in the evening. She felt it sometimes when they lay in bed next to each other in the dark. Something was weighing on Alex's mind and she wouldn't say what it was.

Should Erin ask? She had been debating with herself for weeks. She had asked Alex if she was okay and it only prompted Alex to push the pretense of everything being normal. There was something she was keeping from Erin, and Erin needed to know what it was.

Audrey ran up to Erin, jumping at her and almost bowling her over. Audrey didn't know her own strength. Erin rolled to the ground with Audrey and played with her in the grass, wrestling her. She laughed as the big dog licked her, covering her in drool. Lately she felt closer to Audrey than she did to Alex, and that scared her.

Erin was being driven to meet Alex in London for dinner. Alex had been working on plans for Rainbows at the charity's head office. Erin had been at home doing very little, as usual. They were supposed to meet at Nobu, an exclusive Japanese restaurant in Mayfair. It was Alex's favorite and Erin couldn't deny that the food was beautiful.

Whether Erin liked it or not—and she still didn't—she was accompanied by one of Alex's security team as the black Range Rover pulled up on Berkeley Street, right outside Nobu. She got out and walked to the restaurant entrance. Erin still couldn't get used to having security follow her. She gave her name at the desk and was quickly escorted through the restaurant to a small, private room off the main dining area that was beautifully set and already busy. They brought her a drink and she sat and waited, as she often did, for Alex.

Alex swept in, twenty minutes late. She wore a big, dark-red coat and her hair looked ruffled from the wind. Her cheeks were slightly flushed. She looked exquisite. Erin felt a shiver run through her body when she saw her. She still couldn't help the pure, raw reaction her body had to Alex. Every time. Alex leaned in and kissed her. Her lips were cold, but her kiss was heated. Alex's kisses were always heated. They were never just perfunctory. Alex kissed with the promise of more every time. Erin swallowed the desire that shot to her groin.

Alex threw off her big coat and was suddenly tiny again underneath. A waiter was there immediately to collect her coat and pull out her chair for her.

"We will have a sashimi selection, rock shrimp tempura, edamame and miso black cod. I'll have a sparkling water with fresh lime and ice. Thank you. Please leave us," Alex directed the waiter confidently, and then immediately started telling Erin about her day. Erin was used to Alex taking control and ordering for her, and most of the time it saved her at the posh restaurants that Alex was used to frequenting. Erin would have had no idea what to order, plus she enjoyed Alex's excitement as she showed Erin new foods.

Erin remembered how excited Alex had been to have her taste Nobu's famed miso black cod for the first time, only a couple of weeks ago. They had been at this very table and Alex had had her close her eyes and open her mouth, and Alex had fed the cod to her in forkfuls. It tasted salty yet sweet at the same time, like ribbons of silk in her mouth, and it was entirely irresistible. Alex had squeaked with excitement as she watched her taste it. Alex had made Erin keep her eyes closed the whole time and fed her every mouthful. It was one of the most erotic, non-sexual things Erin had ever experienced.

Tonight, Erin watched as Alex spoke animatedly about her day. The food arrived and they ate as Alex continued to speak. She was so passionate about this project and the difference she could make, and Erin loved seeing her like this.

Things had been weighing on Erin's mind, though, and she had kept quiet about that for too long.

"Alex, I need to know what happened during the meeting with your father. I know you have been keeping things from me, and it shouldn't be like that. If you have an important reason to keep it from me, then I will try to respect that. But mostly, as my partner, you should always be open with me. I love you. I want to be there for you in every way. Whatever it is, please tell me. I never want you to feel like you can't talk to me." Erin reached across the table across the empty plates and took Alex's hand. It was small and delicate in her own. Alex's nails were short and had been neatly manicured by Alicia in a pale pink. Alex looked scared for a moment, just a moment, and then she gathered herself and chose her words carefully.

"I didn't want to tell you, only because I love you and I don't want you to worry about me. But there is a threat. On my life."

"What the fuck?! Alex! Why would you not tell me something like this? This is huge—I'm your ex-bodyguard, for fuck's sake. I am your girlfriend. I should know!" Erin couldn't help her reaction.

Alex continued to speak completely calmly. "This is exactly why I didn't tell you. I knew how you would react. You care too much. My father's head of security thinks I am an assassination target from the same people who are behind the protestors we keep seeing. They think it is a political move to assassinate me and then to move Prince Arthur, my father's younger brother, to the throne. They are investigating. Hopefully they will be able to shut it down."

"I can protect you. I can help protect you." Erin was earnest and insistent.

"Erin, the days when you could act professionally around me are long gone. We both know that your feelings toward me will make it impossible for you to act rationally here." Alex squeezed Erin's fingers in her own. "Erin, I love you, but you are my girlfriend now, not my bodyguard, and you need to learn that."

Erin fought her emotions but couldn't contain them. "And what is life as your girlfriend? I never see you any more. I don't have anything of my own anymore. I can't even go out and do normal things because of who you are. I have to go everywhere with security instead. I'm just like Audrey. I'm like a fucking dog, sitting waiting at home for you, desperate for any attention. Fuck . . . " Erin snatched her hand away from Alex's and put her head in her hands on the table. "I know you warned me about this. I know I chose to give up my freedom for you. But I just didn't realise it would suck this much, you know?"

Erin heard Alex's chair move as she stood up and spoke painfully, but calmly. "Erin, I'm sorry. I'm so very sorry you are finding this so hard. But this isn't the place for this discussion. We are too public here." Alex waved a waitress over. "Please get our coats and inform our security team. Unfortunately, Sergeant Kennedy is feeling a little unwell, so I will be taking her home."

The waitress nodded and curtseyed awkwardly,

giving it her best. "Of course, Your Highness." She scuttled off to do Alex's bidding.

Erin felt herself falling apart. She looked into Alex's eyes. "I don't know if I can do this," Her voice cracked.

"Erin, I love you. I will do whatever is best for you. Hold this together until we get home, please. You will want this to be kept quiet from the people in this restaurant and from our own staff. I promise you, this is what you want. There are ears everywhere." Alex was the picture of calm as the waitress made it back with their coats, helping Alex to dress.

Alex took Erin's arm, firmly. "Walk me out of here and smile," she leaned up and whispered in Erin's ear. Erin felt Alex's lips at her ear and it sent shockwaves of desire through her again. She didn't want them right now. God, her life would have been so much easier if she hadn't fallen in love with a bloody princess. Princess fucking Alexandra, the most famous princess in the world.

She took a deep breath and walked Alex out, arm in arm with her. Photographers snapped as they left. Erin put on her best forced smile.

The drive home felt like it took forever. She sat in silence with Alex's hand firm on her thigh.

Was this what she really wanted? A relationship where the public's perception was more important than talking about the things that mattered?

Alex, you drive me crazy.

Back at home, they undressed quietly and separately. Alex showered while Erin put on some pajamas. Being naked in bed tonight just felt too vulnerable. She got under the covers and sat up against the headboard. Audrey had chosen her own bed for a change, and was snoring away. Erin watched as Alex wandered back into the bedroom, padding softly on the carpet, her body as graceful and lithe as a dancer's under the big, fluffy white towel that wrapped around her. Her hair was wet and combed back from her face. Her eyes glanced up to Erin's and they were vibrant blue in the lamplight.

She shrugged out of the towel and let it drop to the floor. Her skin was pale and smooth like butter. Her breasts were high and round, and the lines of her body were as elegant as ever. Erin couldn't take her eyes off her. Alex climbed into the big bed next to her, knelt at her side, and took her hand. Alex lifted Erin's hand to her lips and kissed it gently. "Erin, I love you so very much. I am so, *so* sorry for not having been open with you. I have thought about this on the way home and I realize I should have told you earlier. I am so used to being alone and thinking just for myself that I selfishly did the same thing again. But I realize that if I want to have a partnership with you, I need to speak openly with you. We need to be a team. If that is still what you want?" She raised her eyes to Erin's and paused for a couple of seconds, giving Erin a window to protest—but not too much of one.

Erin wanted to agree, but she also didn't. She wanted Alex. She couldn't be without Alex now; they had come too far and had been through way too much for a relationship that was so young. Erin knew in her heart that the only way was forward, through it, together.

Alex continued, "In the spirit of full disclosure, my father and I also talked about my relationship with you and my thoughts about our future." Erin raised her eyes for the first time, curious about what Alex would say. "We talked about the possibility that we might marry one day, and what that might look like. We also discussed whether we might have children one day and what that might look like. Erin, I'm not asking you to marry me right now—things are still young between us and we don't need further pressures—but I would like to discuss this with you. Hypothetically, is marriage something you might want one day? How about children?"

Erin wondered if Alex was aware of the great power she possessed to influence and persuade. Erin thought perhaps she was. If the power of her words weren't enough, Erin thought it was no accident that Erin had chosen to kneel next to her entirely naked to have this conversation. It didn't matter though, because Erin adored Alex—the great power of her words, the power of her naked body, and everything else about her.

"I mean, um, I hadn't hugely thought about marriage, I'm not sure it matters to me either way. If it was important to you, absolutely. I guess I always wonder with you . . . . I know there is so much that goes on in your head and so many complications that guide your life and therefore our relationship, that I always wonder what our relationship has the potential to be. I'm in it, Alex, completely. Yes, I'm struggling with everyday life. I'm struggling with the fact that you are a potential assassination target and that I know you will continue to put yourself at risk. But I adore you and cannot for one second imagine being without you. So, if you are still sure, if you still want me, then I guess we find a way to figure things out."

Alex leaned over, her nipples prominent in the cool of the evening, and kissed Erin's lips tenderly. "I want you. I want us. I'm one hundred percent in this, Erin. We've come so far and we won't stop now. I want a chance at a future with you. Let's talk realistically about the risks tomorrow. We can meet with Joanne and discuss my security detail, to see if you agree. How about that?"

Erin nodded. She wanted a say in Alex's security—for sure. She would not stand by and watch Alex get into trouble.

Alex's face was inches away from her own and her eyes were earnest and deep, dark blue.

I could lose myself in the ocean of her eyes.

Alex sat back up on her knees. Still nude. Still effortlessly the most beautiful woman in the world. "Would you like children, Erin, one day?"

"I have zero desire to be pregnant or give birth myself, but I would love children. I would love your children, Lex. I would love them and you every day, for the rest of forever."

Alex smiled widely and genuinely. She was sunlight itself. "Really? You would have kids with me? Thank you, thank you, thank you!" Alex jumped and knelt astride Erin, kissing her all over her face. Erin laughed.

Erin thought for a moment before speaking. "I would do anything with you, you know? I guess I want the fairytale with you."

"Mmmm," Alex murmured. "Let me show you how excited I am about our fairytale." Alex started unbuttoning Erin's pajama shirt and kissing her collarbones. "I think I'll be pretty fucking awesome at fairytales," Alex whispered between kisses. Erin laughed and then felt her nipples sharpen under Alex's lips. She lay back and let Alex undress her. The magic of feeling Alex's naked skin against her own hadn't dulled at all since the first time. Neither had the magic of feeling Alex inside her.

Maybe we could have a fairytale, she mused.

6

Alex hadn't been sure about telling Erin everything until she had actually done it, and then it felt so right. It brought back the intimacy and the closeness they had been missing the past couple of weeks. Alex wasn't used to sharing. She had spent her whole life being so cautious, so private and guarded. Her secrets had been buried so deeply that learning to be in a relationship and learning to trust was a whole new world. She trusted Erin—she did. Alex just needed to learn what that meant and how she needed to be.

Their relationship was still really so young, but it bore the huge pressure of who she was and the fact that they couldn't go anywhere without being photographed and written about.

Alex decided to invite Erin along for the fertility appointment. Erin had laughed about it. "What? Are we getting pregnant already? I know I said I wanted kids, but that was quick!"

"No, silly," Alex had nuzzled into her. "We are just getting me checked out again. Checking if my body is still working the right way for having babies. Talking about options, etc. I had my eggs frozen a few years ago, so even if things are drying up in my old womb, we should still be good."

"You are only thirty five; I don't think you'll be shrivelled up inside yet!"

They pulled up outside the back of the clinic on London's famous Harley Street. The consultant was Dr. Anna Keller, originally from Switzerland, but now running a famous fertility clinic for the rich and famous. The clinic had been emptied for their arrival, to preserve their anonymity, and they were swept in through the back doors and straight into Dr. Keller's consultation room. Joanne and the rest of the security team waited outside the consulation room.

"Princess Alexandra, Ma'am, a pleasure to see you again. Sergeant Kennedy, lovely to meet you."

Dr. Keller was well dressed and tall with long, voluminous dark hair. "Okay, Alexandra, today I want to run your bloods and I also want to do a transvaginal ultrasound, just to get a good look inside—if that is okay with you. I have the details of your recent periods; they were sent through to me. All seems normal there, yes? You have no abnormalities that you are aware of?"

The doctor was efficient and capable, and Alex respected that. "No, nothing. And yes, of course—do what you need to do. Erin will stay with me throughout."

"Perfect. Let's get going."

Alex had purposely worn a short-sleeve, loose-fitting dress to ease the whole process. It gave the doctor easy access for getting started. Dr. Keller tightened a rubber band around Alexis arm and then her gloved hands sought out a vein in the inside of Alex's elbow. Alex had always found medicine fascinating, so she watched avidly as the needle pierced her skin with a sharp pain and then her blood started to run out into the tube that the doctor attached. She caught Erin watching.

"Not scared, are you?" Dr. Keller laughed.

"Not at all," Alex laughed. "Just curious. I like watching."

"Well done, by the way," Dr. Keller said as she finished up and released Alex's arm, moving to label the tubes of her blood. "Well done?" Alex said, momentarily confused.

Dr. Keller continued, "Your speech in the summer. Your coming out. You are an absolute inspiration. I can only imagine how tough that was for you. I just thought you should know that you are hugely respected for it—you're an absolutely incredible woman, whom this country is lucky to have. I am honored to be able to help you both. I know things might be tough now, but there is a bright future for you two. The world is changing. It might not feel like it sometimes, and you might feel like the only lesbian couple in the world. But you aren't." She winked at Alex. "We are all right behind you. What you have done is a huge step forward for both feminism and for the lesbian community."

Alex and Erin both laughed. "You are gay too?"

"Oh, of course," Dr. Keller laughed. "All the best women are. My wife and I have been together for twenty-five years. Now, on that note, do you want to slip your underwear off and get up on the bed? You can keep the dress on; we can just push it up."

Alex laughed. She had always liked this doctor. She met Erin's eyes and they shared a smile. She knew this was a lot for Erin, suddenly here at a fertility clinic with a woman she had only officially been dating for six months, to talk about the potential of artificially creating the next heir to the British throne. But like with so many other things, Erin just took it in her stride. She could be so chill about so much, which was something Alex really loved about her. Her face looked noble and intelligent as she watched.

Alex slipped her underwear down and threw it to Erin, knowing it would embarrass her. "Here, look after this," she flirted, and Erin went bright red. Dr. Keller laughed loudly and heartily. Alex got up on the bed and put her feet in the stirrups.

She was slightly turned on by the situation with the hot older doctor and Erin looking so beautifully turned on and embarrassed all at the same time.

She felt the cold of the jelly as the ultrasound transducer was pushed firmly inside her.

"Right, let's have a look inside here, Alexandra. Erin, are you looking after the underwear?"

"Um, yes, doctor," Erin mumbled.

"Perfect!" Dr. Keller said enthusiastically as she

maneuvered the probe slightly inside Alex. "Now, if you look on the screen, I'll talk you through it."

Alex and Erin watched intently as Dr. Keller told them everything she was seeing. Alex felt excited by the whole thing, knowing that one day, one of these scans would show her baby—their baby. She hoped more than anything that Erin would be by her side, holding her hand then too.

"Everything is absolutely normal, Alexandra. Your body is good to go whenever you are. There shouldn't be any problem getting you pregnant, whenever you are ready." She slipped the transducer out of Alex and Alex felt the sudden loss of it. She dried Alex with paper towel, then Alex put her underwear back on.

"So, let's talk about how you want to do it. Do you have your own ideas?" Dr. Keller was straight to the point, as soon as Alex was dressed and sitting down next to Erin.

"Well, we haven't discussed it extensively beyond Erin not wanting to be pregnant. For obvious reasons, I need to produce a blood heir. My thoughts, and those of my father, are that we use a high-profile donor and draw up legal documents. I would want him to come in and give his sample—and then I assume we would come in and you would put it in me?" Her eyes flashed between the doctor and Erin.

"I'm good with that," Erin said straightaway. "I don't mind who the donor is so long as I like him. I guess we can discuss options?"

Alex leaned over and kissed her lightly on her cheek. "Of course, my darling. You will be such a huge part of this."

"I know," Erin said confidently. "I know it will be our child. I'm not worried."

"Well, that is part of the battle, of course. Choice of the donor. But, you know, you can actually do this at home if you want to. It shouldn't be difficult. Alexandra, we will monitor when you are ovulating, and then on the right days, you get the donor to come and *donate*. You can remain in your bedroom and have it brought to you, and Erin, if you want to, I can give you an insemination kit and you can do it. Completely up to you both. It mostly depends on the donor being committed to being available on the right days. Or he can donate here and we can freeze it and then bring it to you at home when needed, if that was your preference."

"I think that would be my preference," Alex said. "I would like to conceive at home, with Erin, and very much without the donor, if it is possible."

"Another thing to consider, every year you wait, your fertility will decline slightly. I can send you over tables showing how it declines with age. You have bought more time with your frozen eggs—but just putting it out there, the next couple of years would be your best option."

Alex nodded and squeezed Erin's hand. "There is one more thing I was thinking about."

"Go on," said Dr. Keller.

"So, if I had one child successfully this way, I was thinking about doing something different for my second child." Alex looked at Erin for a moment. She definitely hadn't discussed this with her, but in the spirit of being open, she continued, "I would like for my second child to use Erin's egg and the same donor sperm as the first child. But I would want to carry it. I want, more than anything, to carry Erin's child. What do you think?" Alex looked to the doctor and Erin cautiously.

Erin didn't say anything so Dr. Keller interjected, "No reason that shouldn't be possible, Alexandra. More tricky, certainly, and we would need to run some checks on Erin too, but there's a high percentage chance that would be possible."

They both looked at Erin.

"Well, I wasn't expecting that," she looked at

Alex, who saw happiness in her eyes. "I would really love that, if it were possible." She smiled and Alex felt overcome with love for her. Alex squeezed her hand. "I can't wait for the fairytale with you."

Alex was in her office at home working on plans for Rainbows. She wanted desperately to ensure LGBTQ education for children in schools. She was working with her assistant, Jess, on a plan for her and Erin to visit a number of schools throughout the country and speak in front of the pupils about their relationship. To teach them about alternative families. Alex was determined to change things for the better.

Her phone rang and a familiar name flashed on her screen: *PRINCE NICOLAS.*

Nicolas was the Swedish prince whom Alex might have married at one point. It would have been a marriage of convenience for them both, that was for sure. But in the end, Nicolas and his kind and understanding nature had helped Alex see that there was a way through, while being true to her sexuality. That perhaps she didn't have to hide anymore and could be with Erin.

Nicolas had been such a good friend to her. In the end, he was ironically the only friend she had ever been entirely honest with. He understood her. She had maintained her friendship with him and Erin had come to like him as well when she realized what a great guy he really was.

"Nicolas, good afternoon to you. To what do I owe the pleasure of this phone call?"

"Alexandra, lovely to hear your voice. Well, partly, I will be spending a few weeks in London soon and I would love to spend some time with you and Erin. And also, I just wanted to catch up—as your friend—and offer you a listening ear. I know it cannot have been easy, the adjustments you have both made during the past few months. How are things going?"

Alex smiled to herself and wandered out of her office to find a private room for her phone call. It was so kind of Nicolas to check in with her like this. He was right; it wasn't easy. Alex settled into a big chair in one of their reception rooms, after having closed the door. She wanted her privacy.

"Well, I have to say, you were right before and you still are. You were right to tell me to go for it with Erin and to come out publicly. But you are also right in thinking that this path has not been without its challenges. It's tough. I feel such a weight lifted once I came out publicly. I cannot thank you enough for helping me give myself permission to do that. It feels like I was holding my breath for so many years. Hiding something so big.

But now, I'm finding it hard to be open with Erin and to behave normally in a relationship. I have never had a normal relationship. I have never told anyone the whole truth. It is a real adjustment. I think it's confusing for her too. Erin loves me and trusts me, yet I still find myself keeping secrets from her. I'm trying to get past it, but I have a lifetime of secret-keeping to train myself out of. I know you will understand this."

"That, I do, Alexandra, that I do. It can certainly be a lonely life, can't it?"

"Yes. And people don't see that." Alex paused, "Do you ever desire relationships? I'm so sorry for my ignorance about your personal life. I have been so absorbed in my own issues that I have never really tried to learn about how things work for you."

"Yes, I think sometimes that I could be in a romantic relationship and I do yearn for that closeness. I think it is something I would want. I've actually spent a lot of time trying to learn more about myself over the past few months. Your bravery has inspired me. I thought that perhaps rather than keeping my own secrets so fiercely, I might take the opportunity to learn more about myself and what I might want. To think about whether there is a way to do so openly. I don't experience sexual desire—it isn't something that drives me in any way—but touch and physical closeness with someone I was very close to, I think is something that I would want. I have spent so long shutting all this down. So much that I just wish I had given myself more of a chance when I was younger, or that the world offered us more education and more opportunities to see differing sexualities. What you are doing, both in the visibility of your relationship and also through the work of Rainbows, is huge. You are so inspirational, Alexandra. I mean this in the least patronising of ways, but I am so very proud of you."

Alex smiled to herself. She was so fond of Nicolas. He was such a lovely guy. Alex felt momentary pride about what she had been achieving recently and what she had the potential to achieve. However, a dark cloud hung above it all: the threat on her life, all due to her sexuality and desire to make a difference.

"Do you have anyone, Nicolas, anyone you see as a romantic potential?"

"No. I wish I did. It is just so very hard, because I have to hide my identity. I am in groups online—obviously completely anonymously—and sometimes I feel close to the people with whom I speak online. But I know how different things might be, if they knew who I really am. I actually wonder about coming out publicly. Trying to follow your lead and be the difference in the world. Then I might meet someone amazing who would be with me, but that might also just encourage people to want to be with me because of my status, and I don't want that. I want something real."

"I get that, totally. That is one of the things I love so much about Erin. I feel like she loves me in <u>spite</u> of my being Princess Alexandra, rather than because of it. Erin has never been driven by the desire for money or status. I see every day how hard the pressures of sudden fame are for her . . . . Do you know the gender of the person you might want to be romantic with?"

"I really don't think I would mind. I don't think gender would be important to me. I think it would be far more important that the person loves gaming." He laughed loudly, and so did Alex.

"Well, at least you know what is important to you. I think that is a good place to start. You know, if you ever do want to come out, if you want support, I will be by your side in whatever way would help."

"I know you would. It is hugely appreciated. How is Erin?"

"Honestly, Nicolas, I think she is struggling. I think Erin feels she has lost the role that made up her identity. She has spent years being the best bodyguard she can be, always training for something, and now all that has been taken away from her. She is also struggling due to the loss of her anonymity. But mostly, Erin has no focus. I have Rainbows and I try to involve her, but it is my thing. Although she wants to help, she doesn't want to absorb herself in it like I do. She is at home so much and she has Audrey, but that just isn't enough. It is Erin's birthday soon, and I have no idea what to get her."

"Ah, Alex, she needs a passion in her life. We all do. We need a reason to be. I mean, a big passion of mine is games, but outside of that I like to use my high profile to do good in the world, like you have always done. You are driven by such huge things and that brilliance in you has always been so obvious. But Erin isn't a public face—she will stand alongside you, but you know she will never be someone who wants that and thrives on it like you do. You sparkle for the cameras and the journalists; you always have. Even as a young girl, your big blue eyes and your natural charisma could charm the whole world. That is why you are the nation's sweetheart. But Erin needs something else. What is it that she is passionate about? How can you help her with that? Can you get her something for her birthday that will speak to her passion?"

Alex was thoughtful as she finished her phone call. Suddenly, she had an idea for Erin's birthday and she knew just whom she should contact, to try and make it happen.

Later that evening, Alex was curled up on their big sofa. Erin was lying with her feet across Alex's lap, while Alex casually rubbed her feet. She always craved the physical closeness of Erin and wanted to touch her in some way. Massaging her feet while they watched a movie was something she loved to do. She loved watching Erin's long, muscular legs stretched out over her, in her pajama shorts.

Alex also loved that they had the same taste in films and TV. There had to be a strong female lead, and they both enjoyed thrillers and crime. Alex had always loved watching badass women, and now she couldn't help but glance across the sofa at her very own badass woman. Someone she never thought a princess would be able to have. Yet here she was—her actual girlfriend, Sergeant Erin Kennedy. Strong, physical, and capable of anything. Here she was, relaxing under Alex's hands. Alex smiled to herself.

There was a knock on the door to their living room. Alex looked at her phone. It was ten p.m. She felt really pissed off. Couldn't they just leave her alone for once, so she could have a normal, cozy night in with her girlfriend and Netflix?

"This had better be important," Alex called.

"It's Joanne, Ma'am. I have Rob Greene with me. Can we come in?"

Alex sighed and looked frustratedly at Erin, who paused the movie. Alex took a deep breath. "Give me a minute," she called.

Alex jumped up and grabbed a long silk

kimono that looked significantly more professional than the underwear and big t-shirt of Erin's that she had been wearing. "You happy like that?" Alex asked Erin. Erin shrugged. Alex knew Erin wasn't bothered who saw her in shorts and a t-shirt.

"Come in and have a seat, please," Alex called, as she straightened herself up and put on her professional face.

Joanne and Rob Greene were still in their work suits. They came in and sat on the chairs opposite the sofa.

"Ma'am, Sergeant Kennedy," Joanne nodded to them in turn.

"Ma'am, are you happy for us to speak in front of Sergeant Kennedy?"

"Please do. I have no secrets from Erin."

"Ma'am, we have just arrested some protestors who broke into the estate by scaling the castle walls. Two of them were armed. Unfortunately, there is graffiti outside the walls saying *Kill the Queen*. We have to consider this as a significant threat on your life. We would like you to cancel your engagements and stay home for now, until we have chance to investigate further."

Alex felt Erin take her hand. "Lex, I think it

might be wise to consider this. Don't be reckless right now. You have nothing to prove."

Alex felt her heart beat faster and rage burn inside her. She hadn't come this far to stop now. She wouldn't let these people keep her from all she could achieve.

She stood up, to maximise her height and status, and let go of Erin's hand.

"I won't be cancelling anything. I have school visits lined up over the next couple of weeks. They are very important to me and I will be attending them. I will not back down because of this homophobic, mysogynist bollocks." Alex felt her anger bubbling up, so close to the surface.

"With all due respect, Ma'am—" Rob Greene started.

Alex summoned all the size she could out of her diminutive frame. "Do not *with all due respect* me. I will not be changing my mind. I suggest you do your job and make things more secure. I know there is a risk attached to my name and I will never shy away from that. Now get out so I can enjoy the evening with my girlfriend."

"Ma'am," they both nodded and scuttled out the door.

Erin held her arms out on the sofa and Alex

collapsed into them. "I won't back down. You know that."

"Shhh, sweetheart, I know." Erin kissed the top of her head. "You are very brave and I know you would never give up on what matters to you. But what if I come with you everywhere for now? Like an extra, unofficial bodyguard? I don't like the idea of not being there."

"Okay," Alex sighed, exhausted. "I think that would be okay."

7

It was Erin's birthday. She was up early that morning and out walking Audrey on the estate grounds. Erin liked to do this when she could. She enjoyed the early mornings and the time out in the fresh air with her dog. She enjoyed watching how big their Great Dane pup was getting. Alex had not been in bed when Erin woke, so Erin assumed she was up to some birthday preparations.

It was spring now, and Audrey ran through the grass. There were yellow daffodils everywhere and Erin loved them. Although roses had traditionally been Alex's flower, the bright yellow of the daffodils reminded Erin of Alex. Alex was golden yellow and warm like the sunshine. Like the daffodils that spread across the lawn near the woodland on the estate.

Erin thought about being another year older and realized that it didn't bother her as much as it had in previous years. She had a home and a family now, and even though this was the most complicated relationship she could probably have chosen, Erin was happy to be with Alex. Every year from here on out they would spend together, she hoped.

If only she could shake the loneliness and the lack of purpose that had plagued her recently. Erin was feeling a bit better now that she went everywhere with Alex, but it was Alex's life she was living again. She was back in Alex's shadow, and she knew she needed a life of her own.

It wasn't without its stress, however, being Alex's constant companion again. Alex was choosing to ignore the fact there were threats on her life. She wouldn't even discuss it. She just wanted to plough forward with everything she was doing. The school visits were going well, the children held a curious wonder when they met the two women, and Erin loved to watch Alex interact with them. There could not be a better role model for any child, nor a better ambassador for the

British royal family. But Erin felt a constant, dark cloud hanging over them. There were protestors wherever they went. Often the same ones, but Erin didn't like that you never knew which of them might be dangerous and which ones weren't. How people could have so much hate for two adults who were in love, just because neither one of them happened to be a man, Erin could never understand.

Alex had already done so much for lesbian visibility and popularity. Most of the British people who had loved Princess Alexandra before she came out still adored her—and then, by extension, adored Erin. The fact that Alex was so feminine had helped to challenge stereotypes about lesbians held by the older generations, and the fact that Alex spoke so openly and so well helped with public perception. Erin was so proud of her, but also constantly scared for her. Whenever they were in public, Erin was glued to her side. She was highly trained, and even if they wouldn't let her carry a weapon now that she wasn't officially a bodyguard, there was no way she would stop protecting Alex. Erin knew that she would probably feel this way for the rest of their lives together, this intense need to always protect Alex. The biggest threat to Alex's security was and always had been Alex herself. How driven and headstrong she was. It was a quality about Alex that both attracted and frustrated Erin in equal measure.

The sun was bright this morning. It felt like the beginning of summer although it was only spring, and Erin was excited about warmer days ahead. Excited to spend their first summer together in the grounds of their castle as a little family.

Sometimes she thought about their potential children and then it seemed almost too much to comprehend. Because of who Alex was, the need to procreate had been driven into to her from an early age, so it didn't surprise or faze Erin that they were discussing children already. It <u>had</u> surprised Erin when Alex had said that she wanted to carry Erin's child. That wasn't something Erin had ever considered. In the moment, it had felt like the greatest gift that anyone could ever offer her. That there might one day be a little Alex and a little Erin felt like something magical, and Erin realized that she secretly craved that future.

Erin saw she had lost track of time and started to head back to the castle. She had been out wandering and thinking for an hour. Audrey was the first to spot Alex sitting outside at a little table with a coffee. Alex stood up. She was wearing a short, floaty, floral dress with her hair loose around her shoulders. Audrey ran over to her and Alex fell to the floor, laughing and kissing Audrey.

Erin smiled. Sometimes she was overwhelmed by how much she loved Alex. She couldn't imagine ever being without her.

Alex got up from the floor, smiling, and ran over to Erin. She threw her arms around Erin's neck and jumped up to wrap her legs around Erin's hips. Erin caught her and kissed her, and for a second on that sunny spring morning, it felt like they were the only two people in the world.

"Happy Birthday, Beautiful." Alex kissed her deeply. In true Alex-style kissing, there was intent behind it, and her kiss shot a bolt of desire straight through Erin.

Alex jumped down and grabbed Erin's hand, dragging her across the lawn to the table.

Excitedly, she held up a blindfold. "Let me just put this on you, and then I will take you to your birthday surprise." As usual, Erin gave in to Alex's excitement. She could never say no to Alex. Instead, she sat down in the chair and allowed Alex to blindfold her.

"Perfect," Alex said, as she tightened the blindfold. "You definitely can't see, can you? No cheating, or you will ruin it for me!"

"I promise I cannot see a thing! Where are you taking me?"

"You'll see," Alex said mysteriously, and took Erin's hand again. "Just follow me."

Erin had no choice, so she walked where Alex led. It was completely disorienting, to suddenly be without her vision. She knew they were walking through the castle grounds, but in which direction she couldn't be entirely sure. Alex's delicate hand felt small in her own. After about five minutes they stopped. Erin hated surprises, but she knew how much Alex loved giving them, so she tolerated them. It was worth it to see the absolute joy on Alex's face.

Alex leaned in and kissed her suddenly. "Happy birthday, baby," she whispered in Erin's ear as she pulled the blindfold off.

Erin took a second to adjust her eyes to the light and to recognize where they were. They were at the stables, and ahead of them stood one of the stable girls, holding a stunning white-grey horse. The horse had a big red and gold sash around its neck and someone had written in coloured glitter on the horse's white rump: *Happy Birthday Erin!*

It looked like a child had been set loose with a glitter pen.

Erin smiled and looked to Alex and down at her hands, which she hadn't noticed before held telltale sparkles of glitter. "You did that glitter writing, didn't you?"

"Yep!" Alex grinned widely, proud of her work. "This is Shimmer. She is your birthday present. I know you can ride any of the other horses, but it isn't the same as having your own. And I know you used to love eventing before you were a bodyguard. So, Shimmer is an event horse. Very talented, still quite young but with a good bit of experience. So I was thinking, if you wanted to, you and Shimmer could train and do competitions and stuff. I also got you a trainer to help get you back into it. She's actually an old friend of mine. She will come three times a week and work with you and Shimmer. Again, only if you want to. I really didn't want to overstep; I just wanted to give you something for you. So you have a passion again and you can follow your own dreams, rather than being trapped in mine all the time."

Erin looked at Shimmer. The horse was striking in her elegance. She was tall and rangy, and Erin had no doubt that her talent and experience was as Alex promised. Erin had thought that Alex's other horses were incredible and beautifully bred and trained, but to be given a horse of her very own again was the most perfect thing she could imagine.

"Oh god, Alex. Thank you so much. This is the kindest thing ever. I'll look after her, I promise. I cannot wait to ride her. "

"No time like the present," Alex smiled. "Sara, will you get Shimmer ready for Erin, please? Also, please get Sebastian ready for me."

"No, um, if it's okay, I would like to see to Shimmer myself." Erin walked to Shimmer and Sara handed the lead rope over to her.

Erin looked into Shimmer's big dark eyes. "Hey, girl, so it's me and you now. You think we might get on pretty well?" She stroked Shimmer's big noble face and Shimmer blew her lips. Erin smiled. Alex showed her to Shimmer's stable, where a bridle and saddle in the most beautiful, soft, dark brown leather waited. "Oh, my god. Alex. This is incredible. I don't know how to ever thank you." Erin stroked Shimmer and quietly and instinctively went about putting the bridle and saddle on her.

The stable smelled of the wood shavings that

Shimmer's bed was made out of and Erin was suddenly taken back to the years when she used to work with horses—the many quiet hours she spent in stables with these noble creatures. She felt Alex's gaze on her and turned to catch her eye. Erin saw Alex smiling with pride and joy because her surprise had been a success

As Erin led Shimmer out of the stable, she wasn't even dressed for riding, but she didn't care. Her jeans would do.

"I've never ridden a horse that is wearing glitter before." Erin smiled as she swung her leg over Shimmer's saddle.

"There's a first for everything. I don't think Shimmer minds. She told me she likes glitter and she would like to wear it more often!" Alex smiled.

Alex held her phone up and snapped a couple of photos of Erin and Shimmer. Erin couldn't wait to see what Shimmer could do.

"Can we go to the arena?" Erin asked.

"We can go wherever you like! Sara, come to the arena with us and bring Sebastian," Alex directed and walked with Erin and Shimmer, opening the gate to the big sand arena for them. In this arena, a horse and rider could practice dressage and show jumping. The arena was actually made-up of two big sand arenas linked together. The first was a clear space for practicing dressage and for warming a horse up, while the second was set up with show jumps, with brightly coloured wooden poles that could be lowered or raised as one wished.

Erin walked a lap of the dressage arena on Shimmer's back, appreciating her calmness and lightness in her hands. She squeezed her legs against Shimmer's sides and Shimmer sprung into a trot. Erin could feel the power in every stride beneath her. It might have been a long time since she had ridden event horses, but Shimmer felt so effortlessly classy. Shimmer felt incredible already and was clearly highly trained. She obeyed responsively to the tiny movements of Erin's hands or legs.

Erin felt herself smiling widely. She looked across and Alex was watching her from Sebastian's back. She was still in her little dress, which was exposing a significant length of her smooth thighs, and Erin laughed. "Totally impractical horse-riding clothes there, Princess Alexandra."

"Tell me about it! Literally *so* uncomfortable. I'm going to have sores on the inside of my calves from these stirrup leathers pretty soon! It's just that Sebastian didn't want to miss out. I told him Shimmer was spectacular and he agreed. He wanted to come and watch her with you. He thinks Shimmer is beautiful and wants her to be his girlfriend."

Erin rode Shimmer over to Alex and Sebastian. Shimmer reached her long, elegant neck down to sniff Sebastian's nose. They took a second sniffing each other and then Shimmer whinnied loudly and tossed her head. "She's going to be a challenge, Sebastian!" Erin laughed and cantered a circuit of the arena. Shimmer felt so good, Erin turned her to go through to the show jumps. They were set up pretty low so Erin just steered Shimmer to the first jump to see how she would respond. She cleared it with grace and ease and made short work of the others. A cheer came from the corner. It was Alex, still on Sebastian. He made a good grandstand seat!

Erin saw Sara coming over.

"Great work, Ms. Erin, well-ridden. These jumps looked so easy. You want me to make them higher?"

"Sure, go for it," Erin said and then rode over to Alex.

"She looks magical, Erin. You ride her so nicely," the princess told her.

"Thank you so much. Honestly, this is the best birthday present I have ever had."

"You deserve all good things, Erin. I know it is an extravagant gift, but I'm in a position to be able to give and nobody deserves it like you. You have given me more than you will ever know. Anyway," Alex nodded to the jumps. "It looks like the big jumps are ready for you now. Go and show us how it is done!"

Erin looked around to see that Sara had put the jumps up higher. The last jump, she had made very high. Erin squeezed Shimmer into a canter and they made quick and easy work of the first seven jumps. She turned Shimmer toward the last jump. It was significantly bigger, but Shimmer just lengthened her stride, lifted herself, and made it feel easy. It felt like they were flying. Erin knew she had never ridden a horse of this quality before and she couldn't believe that Shimmer was all hers. Alex knew her so well.

She trotted over to Alex. Shimmer's sides were blowing from the exertion and she was lightly sweating. "Princess Alexandra, would you and

Sebastian like to go on a little walk around the estate with me and Shimmer?"

"Why, Sergeant Kennedy, I cannot think of anything I would enjoy more." Alex's blue eyes glimmered brightly in the sunshine as they headed out of the arena and across the ancient turf.

Erin felt like nothing in the world could touch them.

Erin's new trainer was the former Olympic Eventing Champion, Victoria Grey-Hughes. Victoria, or Vic as she liked to be called, was efficient and no-nonsense. Alex had actually known Victoria for many years. They had gone to school together, and it was Victoria that Alex had called to find Shimmer for Erin.

Shimmer had belonged to one of Vic's students, who had competed with her to a high level. But following a fall, and having always been an anxious rider, the girl had lost her nerve for the big competitions and had decided to give up.

Vic demanded a lot from Erin, and Erin found herself loving all of it. She had been out of training and eventing for so long. It felt like there was so much to learn and re-learn, and Vic was determined to get Erin up to scratch.

"Shimmer is not the kind of horse that deserves a shit rider, is she, Erin?" Vic would say whenever Erin got something wrong. "Let's not fuck it up here, Erin. A horse like Shimmer deserves better." Vic was clearly from a high-standing family, but she had a mouth like a trucker.

And Vic was right. Shimmer was a superstar, and Erin knew she needed to sharpen up to keep up with her. Erin still had her bravery and a natural talent for riding, but it was the finer points she was missing from so many years away from it. Her dressage riding was plagued with errors, and although her jumping was a lot better, bravery and positive riding could only take her so far. As Vic kept saying to her, "We need some fucking finesse here, Erin!"

Eventing was a sport composed of three phases. Performing well in one—or even two out of three—was never going to be enough for success these days.

The sport had become so much more professional during the years Erin had been away, and she knew she had a lot to learn.

The three phases of Eventing are dressage, cross country jumping, and show jumping. Dressage asks for skill, high training and elegance from horse and rider; it is like a complex dance with detailed steps. Cross-country jumping demands speed and bravery from both horse and rider. And show jumping requires precision and careful jumping. Shimmer obviously had a load of natural talent and experience in all three. Erin certainly didn't, particularly not recent experience, but she felt her old competitive streak coming back. She wanted to learn and she wanted to be the best rider she could be.

Vic had originally agreed to three lessons a week, but had later agreed to come in five days a week instead. Erin knew she needed help if she wanted to be better.

First thing every morning, Erin liked to come to the stables and ride. Alex was right—it had given her focus and passion. She adored Shimmer and every morning she spent with her, even if she did need some *fucking finesse*.

8

King George had arranged a dinner so the family could meet Erin. Alex knew her mother would be there too, although she had never felt more distant from her mother. Alex knew that her mother had disagreed with her decision to come out, but that she'd had to go along with whatever the king decided. And he had been supportive of Alex.

Alex knew that some of her parents' friends had also been invited, so she was feeling a certain amount of pressure that night. Although she wasn't worried about the event, Alex knew it would be a challenge for Erin and she wanted to protect her.

Things had been running smoothly lately with

the Rainbows school events and Alex was happy about her decision to go ahead with them. There had been protestors for sure, as well as some level of abuse every time in public these days, but Alex stayed above it. And Erin was right by her side. She never left her. Alex knew that Erin still felt like it was her job to protect Alex. Although that made Alex feel safe, she also wished Erin didn't feel she had to carry that constant burden on her shoulders. Erin should be able to feel as free as she could—as Alex's girlfriend, rather than her bodyguard.

Alex had been so very happy after Erin's birthday. Shimmer had been the best birthday present ever and Alex loved how Erin had taken to her immediately. Alex had been unsure whether her old school friend, Victoria, would get along with Erin. Vic was certainly blunt, and not everyone enjoyed that style of teaching. But it so happened that Erin got along with her right away.

Erin seemed passionate about learning everything she could from Vic's immense knowledge pool. She wanted to be the best rider she could for Shimmer.

Many mornings, whenever she could, Alex would sneak down to the riding arena with Audrey and watch. She loved seeing Erin ride, watching her long legs control Shimmer. She loved it when they were jumping and she saw the rush of joy on Erin's face when Shimmer flew over any jump put in front of her. She also enjoyed Vic's snarky one-liners and how she constantly pushed Erin to be better.

Erin never complained. If she had to practice something a thousand times, then that is what she did.

Alex had invited both Vic and Prince Nicolas to the family dinner. She thought a couple of friendly faces might make things easier for Erin.

Alex and Erin arrived at the London palace, where the king was holding the dinner. Erin was sleek in top-to-toe black, with her hair in a neat up-do. Alex couldn't help looking at her when she looked like this. She was still in awe of how handsomely beautiful Erin was, with her hair pinned back from her face and a black silk button-down shirt and jacket. Erin could wear black, and her dark eyelashes, eyebrows and hair just looked bolder and more striking. Alex kissed her before they left the car. "I'm so proud to be with you. I cannot wait to show you off to everyone."

They headed into the palace holding hands.

Into the big dining room where everyone was gathered. Soon enough, they were drinking and socializing, and Erin was holding her own.

Erin's parents were there. Erin's father was polite, but didn't say a lot. Alex had found it easy to talk to him and he seemed honored that she made an effort with him.

Erin's mother was full on. She was over-excited by the occasion and more than a little drunk. Alex could see that Erin was mortified by her, but Alex knew it was just the way family was sometimes. Alex's mother was a lot, but nothing Alex couldn't handle. She posed for numerous selfies with her, so her mother could show her friends.

Alex laughed when she saw the king being pushed to pose for selfies with her. She supposed that they were his first selfie experiences.

Alex's father had made a special effort to talk to Erin. Whatever they were talking about, he was soon laughing loudly and good naturedly. Alex had been surprised by her father's huge support of her over the last year. Surprised—yet at the same time, so very grateful.

Alex's mother made little effort. She seemed to make little effort with everything these days, so Alex, in return, made little effort with her.

Nicolas had been his usual polite, respectful, and well-liked self.

Vic was another surprise for Alex. They had actually been good friends at school and—an exclusively elite, very expensive boarding school. Alex had known no different, but she now recognized that boarding school is an unnatural environment for children. She still vividly remembered being shipped off to school at six years old, where she lived seven days a week during term time.

She had never been close to her mother, but she had felt close to her grandmother, whom she had missed terribly while she was away at school. Erin realized that being at boarding school forced an unnatural level of independence from an early age, and could still remember the trauma of feeling so abandoned.

But Vic had been there at school with her. She had been gregarious and outgoing, and usually up to no good. Actually, there were times during her teenage years when Alex had had a huge crush on Vic. She had never dared act on it though.

"So, lezzy now, are we, Princess? I never called that one." Vic didn't hold back and Alex's eyes widened, hoping nobody else at the party was listening. Vic had always jokingly called her

Princess, and she was probably the only person Alex would tolerate calling her that.

"Well, yes, Ms. Grey-Hughes. That is one word for being in love with a woman." Vic was liberally enjoying a large glass of red wine. Alex, as always, was a cautious drinker.

"I'm just teasing." Vic laughed. "Don't stress! Erin is great. Honestly, she is. She will actually make a very fine rider once I am done with her. I have high hopes for what Erin and Shimmer will be capable of. And what the two of you have done together is huge, both for women and LGBT. I've slept with women, you know?"

"Have you?" Alex couldn't have been more shocked. She wasn't expecting Vic to say that, but then she remembered that when they were in school together, Vic was always shocking her.

"Yes! A few. I wouldn't count it out, you know, in the future. I'm very open to whatever happens—so honestly, I think I am bisexual. It isn't a secret. It is so much more common than you think, Princess. I'm so sorry you felt like you couldn't be open about it sooner."

"You and me, both. I wish I had felt able to be open. I wish I hadn't felt the pressure and the weight of my position in the world as I did. You haven't had a serious partner then?"

"Oh, there have been a few boyfriends, then the flings with women, but no, nothing serious. The horses have always been the main thing for me. You are lucky you found love. Hold on tight to it. Not everyone does."

"Oh, I will! I'm holding on very tight."

Alex looked across the room at Erin, who was still with her father. The light fell beautifully across the sharp lines of Erin's face.

I'm holding on very tight to love.

On the way home from the dinner, Erin and Alex were in the back of the Range Rover, chatting about the evening. Alex was pleased with how well it had gone, and she loved how positive Erin was about it.

"God, I'm so sorry about my mum!" she said. "I loved your dad, you know. He wasn't bad, for a king. A pretty inspirational guy, as it goes!"

Alex laughed and leaned in to Erin. She smiled as Erin's arm slipped around her shoulders. "Yes, we aren't close, but I know what you mean. He is a leader and a performer. I get those qualities from him, definitely."

"And luckily, your beautiful face is the only thing you inherited from your mother, so it seems. Phew, you were right; she was hard work. She was so frosty."

"She has *always* been frosty. She was a suitable person for a king to marry. That is how it went. They live entirely separately and have for many years, although obviously nobody knows that. In public, they appear enough together. Enough so that nobody thinks any differently. Even my mother can plaster a smile on for a couple of hours."

Erin pulled Alex closer to her. Alex could never get enough of Erin's strong arms around her.

"It was nice to see Vic socially tonight. Makes a change from her shouting at me when I'm losing Shimmer's outside shoulder in a half-pass! She is really fun. Oh, and she LOVES her wine, doesn't she?"

"It's actually so great to get to know her properly again. That was what she was like when we were at school. I used to crush on her a bit when we were teenagers, you know?"

"I bet you did, Princess." Erin smirked at her in the dark.

"Oh, don't you start calling me *Princess* too. You heard her doing that, I guess?"

"Yes, it was funny. She does make me laugh. Nothing ended up happening between you and her?"

"No, it was silly, really. She was my friend. She was wild and I think I was jealous that she was able to be wild. I found it attractive. But I wouldn't have dared act on that."

"You told me once about a woman you thought you were in love with . . . years ago. I know I never really asked about her, but I would like to know if you are happy to speak about her."

Memories of a beautiful summer when Alex was twenty-two years old flooded back to her, as though it were yesterday. "Annabelle," she said. "She is now Lady Annabelle Delacourt. She is Lord Delacourt's wife. They have three lovely children."

"What happened between you and Annabelle?"

"I was twenty-two. She was the same age as me. We had been friends at University. She stayed with me at the palace for the summer. I used to think about her. I had been thinking about her for so long. I had all these feelings that I didn't totally understand, or maybe I chose to pretend that I didn't understand them. She was so beautiful, tall, and athletic. We played tennis together and would ride together. She was an incredible tennis player. She always beat me at tennis, but I didn't mind because whenever it was doubles she chose me as her partner, and then we won. Annabelle always won at everything she did."

Alex paused for a second. It felt like it had happened yesterday. "One day we played tennis in the sunshine against Lord Hugo—and funnily enough, Lord Delacourt. We won and there was a moment where Annabelle swept me up in her arms and kissed me to celebrate our win. The sun was bright and we weren't alone, and it was innocent enough, the kiss. But at the same time, I knew it wasn't innocent. There was an intensity to the way she held me and the heat with which she kissed me that promised more.

I knew in that moment that things between us had changed. That night, Annabelle told me I should sleep in her bed with her, and of course I wanted to—more than anything else, I wanted to. I don't think either of us had a clue about what we were doing sexually, but it felt magical. Feeling her naked body against mine was the most beautiful thing I could imagine. I tasted her and I knew that for me, there was no going back. I had been in love with her for years when I actually thought about it—following her around, quietly loving her—and when she took me sexually, it was all over for me. I loved her. We slept together every night that summer. I moved her into my room. Nobody ever suspected anything. We were both girls, so what could we do? I used to tell her I loved her. She would say, 'I know.' She never said 'I love you' to me.

I had this hope, that what we had could become something more. I had this hope that we could live happily ever after. But at the end of the summer, Lord Delacourt proposed to her. She left me. I broke down and cried and begged her to stay. I begged her for more. She said what we had could never be real and that in the world we lived in, women married men. She said that given who I was, I was ridiculous to think otherwise and did I want the monarchy to become some kind of joke? She said nobody could ever know about what happened between us. She left me and never looked back.

I was distraught, for so long. I learned to accept it, but my walls went up so high that I could never imagine tearing them down again, not until you. When I met you, everything changed for me. You made me believe the life I craved so badly was possible."

Alex sighed loudly and Erin took her chin in her hand and kissed her.

"I'm so very sorry you went through that. My first love was Blake. She was a few years older than me, and I used to think that what we had was very real. I met her when I was working with horses. I was twenty. When we went away to horse competitions and slept in the horse box together, there was this big bed above the cab of the lorry. It was like a den or a nest or something, barely high enough for you to sit up without banging your head. We used to fill it with pillows and duvets and we would sleep up there together. It felt perfect—until it didn't. She ended things with me so she could see one of the other girls."

"You always knew you were gay?" Alex asked her. It seemed strange thinking about a young Erin just wanting to love this Blake. It made Alex feel angry and protective of her.

"Pretty much. I mean, I dabbled a bit with guys

because everyone did, but I felt nothing. I knew it wasn't really me. I used to crush on my English teacher at school. I think I probably knew for sure then. How about you? When do you think you knew for sure?"

Alex contemplated for a second. "I think I was mostly in denial through my teenage years, even when I caught myself looking at Vic when she was getting changed, and fantasizing about her. I still think I just told myself it was a phase or something. Even though I had absolutely no interest in boys. It honestly was the moment that Annabelle picked me up and kissed me on that tennis court in the sunshine, and we were oblivious to the guys. I think I knew for sure in that second that nothing could compare to that feeling."

"So, tell me more about how you used to check out Vic when she was getting changed," Erin said teasingly, lightening the tone.

"Ah, god, don't tell her! Please don't! You know tonight she actually told me she is bisexual. I really wasn't expecting that!"

"So, you could have had a chance with her all those years ago?"

"Maybe so! Might have been more fun than

lying in my little bed touching myself and imagining it was her... although that was pretty fun!"

Erin laughed. "Now, I *wish* I had seen that!" Erin kissed her again and her hand was on Alex's leg, at her knee. It ran slightly up her skirt to her inner thigh. Alex felt flooded by a huge rush of desire for Erin. It was funny how talking about her feelings for Vic and for Annabelle had brought them here.

There was a panel separating Alex and Erin from the driver, and from Joanne in the front. It was soundproofed and Alex was grateful for that. Unless they pressed the intercom, nobody could hear them in the front of the car.

Alex was suddenly lost for words as she felt Erin's hand moving slowly, further up her inner thigh. Goosebumps shot right across her body. Erin's fingers traced patterns lightly across Alex's skin, before her hand grabbed Alex's thigh firmly and possessively and pulled it apart from her other leg. Erin fixed Alex with her gaze, "Is this okay?" she whispered seductively.

Alex nodded. She could see the driver if she looked in the rearview mirror, so he could certainly see her face. But thankfully, he had no chance of hearing her. Alex felt suddenly more turned on than she ever had. She felt lust running through her body and pooling between her legs.

Erin's fingers reached her underwear and brushed against it. Alex's clit jumped immediately at Erin's touch, even through the lace of her panties. Keeping a straight face in case the driver or Joanne realized what was happening was proving to be a challenge. Alex was grateful for the darkness.

"Your underwear is pretty wet, Princess Alexandra, I think you should take it off," Erin whispered. Her eyes were dark with the promise of what was to come.

Alex felt another rush of desire run through her and quickly moved as discretely as she could to shift her hips up. This allowed her to wriggle her panties down over her ass, down to her ankles. Erin reached over and helped pull them off of each foot. Alex's eyes widened as she watched Erin take the small lace thong in her hand up to her face and inhale deeply. "Mmmm," she said. "You smell incredible."

She put the lace thong in the pocket of her jacket and Alex watched her, mesmerised. Her pussy felt suddenly exposed and open without her underwear on. She felt overwhelmed with excitement. She watched as Erin's strong, capable fingers returned to her inner thigh and inched slowly up toward her burning core. Alex found herself hitching her skirt up higher so she could open her legs wider. She needed Erin so badly right now. Erin's fingers finally reached her dark heat and began to rhythmically stroke her, firmly and confidently. Alex found her breath quickening and her body responding instantly to Erin. Her whole body was on high alert, flooded with her sexuality. Erin's fingers continued to work on her, unhurried, playing with her expertly. Alex craved more, overwhelmingly she wanted Erin inside her, but she knew that was nearly impossible without anyone noticing.

"I know you desperately want me inside of you. If you are a good girl now, I'll fuck you properly when we get home. How about that?"

Alex nodded silently. "Mmm," she found herself mumbling incoherently. It was very hard to concentrate on anything while Erin's fingers were toying with her and sliding around her clit.

"Now, I know you told me explicitly about those fantasies of yours—about outdoor sex and sex in public. I was thinking this would be a good start," Erin whispered, her voice dark and silky, like whisky over ice. Alex had indeed voiced those fantasies to Erin. Those and so many others. There had been years of fantasizing and never being able to act on any of it. Suddenly, Erin was giving her all these opportunities.

"Now, we are nearly home. You are going to stop moaning and press the intercom and tell the driver that you want him to drop us in the woodland, and that we will walk home across the estate." Alex hadn't even realized she was moaning. "And then, I am going to fuck you in the woods, just like you have dreamed about." Alex felt herself nearly orgasm there and then at Erin's words, but she pulled herself together. She had wanted this so badly. She wanted to feel the outdoor air on her skin when they had sex. She had wanted to be close to nature. Alex had so desperately wanted to do it outside, under the deep cloak of darkness. They stopped at the castle gates and waited for security to let them in. They were buzzed straight through. Then Alex pressed the intercom. "I'd like you to drop us by the woodland, please. We would like to walk home across the estate." Alex wasn't sure she had managed to control her breathing and the moans that kept escaping her lips.

"Of course, Ma'am," came the driver's response, and he pulled up next to the woodland.

Alex gasped as Erin pulled her hand away from Alex's skirt and opened the car door. Alex sat for a second and closed her eyes as she pulled her skirt back down to a respectable length. She snapped back to life as the door on her side opened. It was Joanne, holding the door open for her as was protocol. Alex stepped from the Range Rover on shaky legs, leaving her jacket behind. Joanne closed the door and the Range Rover drove off.

Fuck, Alex thought to herself. *I hadn't thought about Joanne.*

"Sergeant Davis, Erin and I would like to walk alone. We won't need you."

"Ma'am, I don't think it would be wise for me to leave, just in case." Joanne was persistent. She knew her role.

"Joanne," Alex looked to her, appealing to her with her eyes. "We would very much like to spend some private time and walk through the trees alone, just the two of us. I will have Erin with me. I appreciate that you won't leave, but I would like you to wait outside the woodland, here at this entrance. We won't be long. We will be safe."

Joanne fished into her pocket and handed

Alex the silver bracelet that contained the tracker. Alex knew she was right and slipped it over her wrist. "If there is anything, Ma'am, anything, please just press the alert button. Sergeant Kennedy," Joanne turned to Erin, "Please, don't hesitate to call me if there is anything at all suspicious. I will inform the security team and the grounds team of your location, but that you are not to be disturbed. I'll make sure nobody comes close." Joanne seemed to get what was going on. Alex resented for a second that she was who she was, and that all this was necessary—just so she could go for a walk with her girlfriend in the woods.

Erin nodded to her. Alex felt the cold night air between her legs on her exposed pussy.

Erin took her hand and they headed into the trees.

It was dark in the trees, apart from the moonlight flickering through the leaves. Alex was beyond excited to be totally alone with Erin, and still so turned on. She could feel her own wetness on her inner thigh. God, she needed to feel Erin inside her. Erin led her to a tall tree where moonlight fell across it.

"You want to do this? Are you sure?" she whispered to Alex.

"So sure," breathed Alex. "I'm so excited."

Erin smiled and put her hands on Alex's hips, positioning her with her back against the tree. Alex felt the gnarly tree trunk through the silk of her dress. Erin took each of Alex's wrists in her hands and raised them above her head, pulling them both backwards behind the slim trunk of the tree. Alex gasped as she felt cold metal at her wrists snapping firmly around each one.

"Are they handcuffs?" she asked.

"They are. Police issue handcuffs. I brought a small bag with me, in the car, just in case. Is this all right? Let me know if you are ok with everything."

Alex tested them slightly and they gripped firmly into her narrow wrists. She was completely restrained against the tree and she liked how it felt. "More than ok. I love it. Thank you for doing this for me." It felt so different than any restraints they had used in the bedroom. It felt so thrilling to be out here in the moonlight, restrained against a tree. She watched as Erin moved to the small bag she had brought and pulled out a blindfold, which she put on Alex. Losing her sight made the feeling of the cool breeze on her body more intense. The bark of the tree trunk bit at her back and the sharp metal of the handcuffs bit at her wrists.

She felt Erin's hands suddenly on her body, running down her body over the silk of her dress. She felt her nipples rise to meet Erin's hands. Then she gasped as she felt Erin rip the top of her dress and her bra down, suddenly exposing her breasts to the night air. She felt her nipples tightening as hard as two pebbles and she felt herself twinge desperately between her legs, needing more.

She then felt Erin's hands on the skirt of her dress pushing it roughly up and wedging it just above her ass between the small of her back and the tree. She felt utterly exposed when the cold hit her wetness. She knew Erin would be looking at her body. It was something she had always enjoyed, knowing how much Erin desired her. She remembered the early days when Erin had first started working for her. Erin would look at her sometimes with lust in her eyes, and Alex liked it. She used to dress seductively on purpose when she knew Erin would see her. Erin had never been good at hiding the hunger in her eyes, even when she was her bodyguard, and not her girlfriend.

Erin's hands moved across her body, touching her everywhere. Alex felt herself arching her back into the tree and relaxing into its strength and the unforgiving metal of the handcuffs against her wrists. She ached to feel Erin inside of her.

Finally Erin's fingers moved to tease her folds and slip around her wetness. She leaned in and kissed Alex deeply as she touched her. Her tongue pushed into Alex's mouth and Alex sucked on her tongue, not wanting it to leave. Wanting Erin's tongue to be inside her mouth always.

Erin kept kissing her as she worked her hand between Alex's legs and Alex moved her foot outward, to allow her access. Erin's fingers parted Alex's slick folds and pushed deep and hard inside of her.

Alex gasped into Erin's mouth and found herself moaning loudly. Erin began to fuck her with her fingers as she kissed her. Alex lost any concept of what or how much or how many as she lost herself in Erin's kiss and the feeling of Erin moving so deep inside of her. She felt her body move to receive each thrust of Erin's and she was pinned tightly between Erin's body and hand and the tree and the handcuffs. She felt tightly bound, like she couldn't escape and she was Erin's prey.

Just there for Erin to take, to feast upon her body. She arched her back and ground against Erin's hand. She felt something brushing up firm against her clit. She cried out and lost herself into the deepest and most intense orgasm she could ever have dreamed of. She felt herself gushing her pleasure down the inside of her legs. Her whole body shuddered as wave after wave washed over her, and her legs lost any ability to take her weight.

The next thing she knew was Erin carefully releasing her handcuffs and slowly pulling her arms back to her sides. Taking her blindfold off. Erin tenderly pulling her skirt down and holding her up to keep her from collapsing. She felt like she was still in a dream as Erin put her own coat around Alex and led her home. Alex tried to look some semblance of normal when she saw Joanne, who moved silently into step some distance behind them, but Joanne must have known what they had been up to in the trees. Alex knew she looked anything but normal.

When they got home, Erin ran a bath and lifted Alex into it. Alex felt blissful as the warm bubbles enveloped her. "Are you okay, Lex?" Erin whispered to her.

"Perfect. So perfect. That was incredible. I just

don't have many words." Alex smiled and Erin leaned over the bath, kissing her lightly.

"It's okay, you don't need words. Now, I'm going to wash every inch of you." Erin moved to get a sponge and shower gel. Tenderly, she began to wash Alex's body all over. Alex relaxed into it. Erin shampooed her hair, massaging her head all over, so gently and lovingly.

There were no words, but there didn't need to be as Alex relaxed into the warmth, and the bubbles, and Erin's love.

This is love and this is incredible.

9

After the night in the trees, Erin felt a new intensity to her love with Alex. Alex had spoken to her before about fantasies—there were so many fantasies she had that she had never acted upon. A lot of them were easy, and Erin had no problem bringing them into their sex life.

Alex's fantasy of being properly restrained and dominated had been something Erin had thought about carefully. She had been dominant with previous lovers, and in some ways, it felt natural to her. It felt natural as part of her dynamic with Alex, but she adored Alex so much and Alex was so delicate. Erin had always been so scared to hurt her, or to take something too far. She was afraid because sometimes when fantasies become reality, they might not be what one really wants.

Erin had enjoyed teasing Alex during the car journey. She had loved watching involuntary moans escape the princess's lips, while she tried so desperately to remain silent. Alex restrained against that tree with her breasts exposed and the tight blonde curls between her legs looking almost silver in the moonlight was one of the most beautiful and highly-erotic things Erin had ever seen. She had waited for a minute after Alex had been blindfolded, and had watched her body as her breathing quickened and her breasts rose and fell above her ribcage. Goosebumps raced across her skin in anticipation of Erin's touch and her nipples had been rock hard in the cold air the whole time.

Erin had wanted to devour her in that second, to take her in every way possible. The intensity of connection she felt, as she plunged her fingers deep inside Alex and felt her body respond, was overwhelming.

She was more in love than she had ever imagined was possible.

Alex had fallen asleep on her chest that night and Erin had breathed in the taste of her shampoo on her damp hair as she fell asleep.

The next morning, Alex couldn't stop kissing her. She wanted to talk about it and re-live every second of it. But when Erin had walked her back to the castle and Alex had barely been able to speak, Erin worried for a moment that it had been too much. But the next morning, she had felt reassured. Alex was more alive and animated than ever.

Red marks from the cuffs on her wrists were beginning to change into blue bruises, and Alex loved them. There were scratches on her back from the tree and Alex couldn't stop admiring them in the mirror. She had to hide it all in front of anybody else. But in their own rooms, by themselves, Erin watched as Alex enjoyed the marks that had been left on her body.

The power Erin had over Alex physically was easy to assert. She was much bigger and stronger than Alex, so it made living out these things a lot much easier. Erin had begun to notice how much Alex craved for her to take over—that sexually Alex wanted to lose herself and not to have to make all the decisions.

It was an escape, Erin thought to herself, from the reality of Alex's real life. There, she had to constantly be in control and to lead. It was why she enjoyed submitting sexually to Erin so much more.

Letting Erin dominate her seemed to have brought out a new level of adoration in Alex. Alex nuzzled, kissed, and touched her constantly whenever they were alone—and even sometimes when they weren't. Alex also wanted sex more often, as though it gave her a release from real life.

Erin still felt the weight of the threats on Alex's life and the increased security wherever they went. They had had further meetings with Rob Greene and Sergeant Davis, and although they were arresting people and investigating where they could, they couldn't stress enough how great the risk was and would the princess *please* consider taking fewer risks. Of course, Alex still wouldn't take their advice. Erin could only imagine how the threats weighed on Alex too, but she wouldn't speak about it. She would never say she was scared. She would just lose herself to Erin sexually, or sometimes she just wanted to be wrapped up and hugged and loved. Either way, Erin gave whatever was needed from her.

When she saw creases of worry on Alex's lovely face, she would wrap Alex up in her arms and hold her tight, kissing her head and telling her everything would be okay.

When Alex nuzzled into her and started kissing her, Erin knew what she needed and how she needed to feel taken, to feel release. She would throw Alex onto her back and get on top of her, and give her the release she craved so badly. Then afterward, she could wrap Alex in her arms again and kiss her and kiss her and kiss her some more and wish that her kisses and her love would be enough to protect her.

Everywhere Alex went in public, Erin stuck to her like glue. Erin spent her time on high alert and never separated from her.

Alongside the new intensity to their love, running deep just below the surface, was the fear they were both feeling. Erin knew she was absolutely terrified of something happening to Alex.

A few weeks later, Erin had her first competition with Shimmer. Vic had conceded that her riding was getting *significantly less shit* and she had declared that Erin and Shimmer should begin to enter competitions. The competition itself was at a lower level than Shimmer was used to, due to Erin's lack of recent experience. Usually, a horse with as many competition points as Shimmer would be banned from a novice competition, but they ran an "open novice" class to take into account riders trying to get more experience.

Erin felt nervous on the morning of the competition. She had bathed Shimmer the day before in purple shampoo, which really made her glow white. She looked dazzling in the sunshine. Then she had been up early that morning to plait Shimmer's mane and tail herself. Obviously, the stable girls had offered to do it for her, but she hadn't wanted them to. Erin enjoyed the quiet hours to herself in the stable with Shimmer. There was something so calming about hearing Shimmer munching on hay as Erin plaited her mane into fifteen little plaits and then rolled each one up into a tiny ball and secured it with a needle and thread.

They had all travelled together in the horsebox. Erin, Vic, and Shimmer—and obviously Sara, the stable girl. Vic drove the horse box, wielding the huge lorry as though it were a tiny car. Of course. She rode a fine line between terrifying and reassuring with her driving. A certain amount of confidence was surely needed to drive a lorry of that size. Vic was obviously not short of confidence.

Alex came too, even though she had been asked not to by security, and Erin was torn. She loved having Alex's absolute support, but at the same time she worried about Alex's safety, and she didn't want to be thinking about that when she was trying to focus on riding.

It was finally agreed that Alex would go in disguise as a stable girl. Alicia had helped Alex with her disguise. When Erin saw her, she was shocked. She barely recognized Alex in jeans that were too big for her, a blue polo shirt, and short, ankle-length riding boots that were scruffy leather. She had on a wig that gave her a mousy brown, frizzy, bushy ponytail. Alex also had brown contact lenses in, and glasses on, and no makeup. Alex walked differently, she held herself differently, and she spoke differently.

She looked a million miles away from Princess Alexandra. Erin had always thought Alex was a gifted actress. It was amazing how much of Princess Alexandra's instantly recognisable face was tied up in her expensive-looking, ashy blonde bob, her dazzling blue eyes, and the dresses and heels she always wore. Without them, she looked like a different person entirely. She looked plain, and it amazed Erin that someone with looks as striking as Alex could ever look plain.

She laughed as she saw Sergeant Davis also dressed as a stable girl. Joanne Davis was a lot less talented an actress. She looked serious. She looked wooden. She still looked one hundred percent like a police officer.

It reassured Erin, though. Nobody would look twice at the stable girl with the frizzy hair suspecting it might be Alex. Not for a second.

The day went smoothly and Shimmer was every inch the superstar that Erin had known she could be. The nerves quickly disappeared as Erin's muscle memory kicked in. Riding Shimmer through the three phases of the event felt as natural and easy as it had at home. Even when she was in the dressage arena by herself, she could hear Vic's words in her head. *More leg, more fucking leg. Forward from your seat. Light in your hands.* Shimmer had danced across the beautiful green turf as elegant as a dancer. Erin had remembered all the movements.

Erin almost laughed in the next phase because still she could hear Vic with her during the show jumping course. *Take your time on the bend. Don't fuck this up!* Shimmer made light work of the brightly-colored wooden poles, jumping each one neatly and carefully.

Then an hour later, on the cross-country course with hedges and ditches and water to splash through, there were miles of open countryside ahead of them. *Push on forward after each jump. Don't be a ditherer. Every moment you dither is a second slower, and slow horses don't win.* Erin felt the wind rush in her face as Shimmer galloped up the final hill. Shimmer was still so powerful and strong underneath her. Erin saw the last jump appear and Shimmer clocked it at the same time. She felt Shimmer beneath her assessing it herself, lengthening her stride and flying over it as easily as if it had been a twig on the floor. Then across the finish line.

What an incredible horse.

There had been Alex with her frizzy wig and glasses, waiting next to Vic at the finish line and smiling widely at her. "You were fucking awesome right there, Sergeant Kennedy!" she called out in a voice that sounded a million miles away from Alex's usual extremely posh, carefully considered words. Erin smiled as she jumped down from

Shimmer's back and checked in with Vic. "Shimmer, she was amazing! Seriously, what a horse."

Vic smiled knowingly at her. "I know Shimmer is amazing. That's why I chose her. You did all right yourself, Kennedy. You didn't fuck it up. You won, you know. I'm pretty sure. You were in the lead before the cross country and by my timings you got no penalties on the cross-country course."

Erin felt sheer joy run through her and she kissed Shimmer on the nose. "Well done, girl. We fucking won!" Erin turned to the others, "Have we got any champagne in the horsebox? I think this is cause for celebration!"

They had all laughed and had a drink together as Sara washed the sweat off Shimmer and took her for a walk to eat some grass. The early summer sun began to lower in the sky.

It wasn't till they got home and Alex stripped off her frizzy wig and glasses that she finally kissed Erin properly.

"Congratulations, babe. I am so very proud of you. You were outstanding today! Vic will never say it to you, but she thinks you have real potential, you know?"

"Does she really? You've just made that up." Erin laughed.

"No, I'm serious! She thinks you are good!"

"You looked so unlike Princess Alexandra today; it was crazy. I barely knew it was you."

"Well, that's the idea, right? I can sneak along to your horse competitions with you and nobody will have any idea it is me."

Erin smiled. "That is the idea, yes. I loved having you there and even more than that, I loved not being worried about something happening to you. Because, honestly, I am worried, you know."

"Honestly, I am a bit scared too."

Erin smiled weakly at Alex's admission. It was the first time she had said the words. Erin took her in her arms and held her close. "I've got you, Lex, I promise. I won't let anything happen to you."

10

The weeks went by and nothing bad happened, but living with the fear that it might had begun to weigh on Alex's mind. Her favorite days were horse competition days, with Erin, Shimmer, and Vic. There was a real freedom to dressing up as someone else for the day. Every weekend they had been doing it ,and still nobody had recognized Alex. Not even people she knew. Alex's own cousin had come to congratulate Erin and to introduce herself, and she hadn't noticed Alex. There was a certain anonymity to being a stable girl, Alex had noticed, which let her just skate along under the radar. That suited her on so many levels. At Erin's horse competitions it was about her and Shimmer. If Alex had attended as herself, it would have immediately become "The Princess Alexandra Show" and Alex wanted so badly for Erin to have this thing for herself.

It was going so well. Week after week, under Vic's consistent guidance, Erin and Shimmer won or placed highly in everything they entered. They moved up to a higher level and they kept doing well. It was a delight. Every weekend was wonderful and Alex loved each second of their trips out, supporting Erin and Shimmer. She loved to bring her camera and take photos and videos of them. The joy on Erin's face when she was riding filled Alex with warmth. Erin had a happiness now that Alex hadn't seen in her before.

The previous weekend, Erin and Shimmer had qualified for the National Championships. It would be a big step up for them, but Vic had declared that they were ready.

Tonight, Erin and Alex were attending a private party at the home of one of Alex's old friends. A lot of people Alex knew would be there. The very wealthy and the British nobility. Vic was there. She was from a hugely wealthy family, she was an Olympic champion, and she loved a party. Vic seemed to have an invite for any and every party.

Alex had on some level already known that Lady Annabelle Delacourt would be there, but had not exactly prepared herself for it. As soon as she walked in on Erin's arm, Alex saw Annabelle across the room. Annabelle had always been eye-catching, tall, and athletic. Her hair was dark blonde and carefully curled around her shoulders. She wore a deep red dress, and three children seemed to have taken no toll on her body.

Alex had seen her at parties like this a few times over the years, but this was the first time she had seen Anabelle since she had been with Erin.

She wished she didn't still react when she saw Annabelle, but she did. Annabelle was her first love and every time since, these overwhelming feelings rushed through her body when she saw her.

It was complicated and things were so different now. She loved Erin, absolutely and completely, and she had no doubts. Still, that didn't stop these uncomfortable feelings from surfacing around Annabelle.

Erin was quickly dragged off on Vic's arm to meet some horsey people, and Alex found herself momentarily alone after having been thrust a glass of champagne from a passing waitress. Then, exactly as Alex knew would happen, Annabelle swept over in a burst of strong perfume and swooped her arms around Alex.

"Alexandra, so lovely to see you. You look stunning. I always loved this blue on you. It brings out your eyes."

Alex felt engulfed by her. She felt small and fragile and twenty-two again.

"So, I hear things have changed since I saw you last, Alexandra." Annabelle had always used her full name. Alex used to like hearing the way the syllables of *Alexandra* moved around Annabelle's red lipsticked mouth, but now it made her feel a bit sick.

"Your public coming out was bold, but right. Times have indeed changed." Annabelle took Alex's hand in her bigger hand and fixed her eyes on Alex's. "I know you have this thing of sorts, with your bodyguard, but I think you should expand your mind to other options." Annabelle's other hand moved to Alex's ass. Alex flinched at the touch. "We had something really special. I'm sorry I was too immature to realise it at the time and to be the partner you deserved. Well, things have changed now. Imagine the two of us together. I would leave Rupert for you, Alexandra. It has always been you that I loved. You know that, don't you? You could be queen and I could be by your side." Annabelle was so close and the room felt like it was closing in on Alex. It felt like nobody else was there, apart from the two of them. Alex felt lost for words and young and naive again, like she had been when she had fallen in love with Annabelle.

Annabelle's hand moved up to the curve of her hip. "You look a bit pale, Alexandra, are you feeling okay? You should come outside." Annabelle, with one hand on her hip and the other pulling her hand, moved Alex toward the door as if she had been a child. Alex felt suddenly powerless and terrified. Her eyes darted around the crowd and suddenly caught Erin's.

She knew how responsive Erin was to just a scared look from her, so it was only seconds before Erin appeared at her side. Alex threw herself dramatically at Erin, wrapping her arms tightly round Erin's waist.

Erin's strong arm was around her instantly and Annabelle's hands were no longer on her body.

There was a moment where Erin and Annabelle, both tall and sure of themselves, faced off against each other like two prowling lions shaking their manes.

"I'm Sergeant Erin Kennedy." Erin smiled falsely and extended her hand, while still gripping Alex tightly with her other arm.

"Your reputation precedes you, Sergeant Kennedy. I'm Lady Annabelle Delacourt. A pleasure to meet you, I'm sure." Privilege dripped from Annabelle's voice like the diamonds that hung from her earlobes and wrist.

Alex clung tighter to Erin.

"The princess isn't feeling so well. She has had a long day, so I'm going to take her home," Erin said boldly.

Alex smiled inside, desperately grateful to Erin for making the decision for her.

"Goodbye, Lady Delacourt."

"Goodbye, Sergeant Kennedy. I hope you feel better soon, Alexandra." Annabelle hung Alex's name in her mouth, as she drew it out in her most seductive voice.

Alex didn't even look up. She felt herself being ushered straight outside by Erin.

"Are you okay? Did she hurt you? What happened?" Erin was earnest in her desperate care for Alex.

"I didn't do anything. I promise, it's you I love, it is you I want." Alex felt panicked and sick.

Erin pulled her in close. "I know, Lex, I know. I'm not worried about that. I'm worried about you."

"She didn't hurt me; she just said some things. Can we go home? Please."

"Of course. I've got you, my darling. I've got you. I promise." Alex nuzzled into Erin's arms as Erin summoned Joanne, who was waiting close by.

"Princess Alexandra is feeling a little unwell. Have the cars come immediately and have someone run a bath for when we get home, and deliver some sushi to our rooms."

Alex felt so protected and safe in Erin's arms. She allowed herself to be enveloped into the warm cocoon of Erin, who rocked her in her arms like a baby all the way home.

"How are you feeling?" Erin asked her the next morning, as they sat outside with their coffees, enjoying the sunshine.

"I'm all right now. Thank you for saving me last night. I think I had underestimated the amount of power that Annabelle has held over me for so long. For so many years I had craved her love. For so many years I had dreamed about the day that she would leave her husband and come for me. I had fantasized that our love meant as much to her as it did to me. I think the whole time I had seen her through rose-tinted glasses. But last night, I saw who she really was and it made me feel sick in the very pit of my stomach. Annabelle doesn't love me. She never has. She wants to be with me now because of who I am, and who I will become, and because my coming out has actually had an overwhelmingly positive public response. Annabelle is a social climber. She was friends with me years ago because of who I was and whom I could introduce her to. Now, when I think about it, I think Annabelle knew that I was in love with her all along. She only slept with me so she could further abuse her power over me. Ugh, I'm so sorry. You don't need to hear all this." Alex put her head in her hands.

Erin reached out for her, took her hands away from her face, and tenderly cupped her chin. "Lex, we are a team now. It's you and me, always. Nothing you can say will change the way I feel for you. We all have a past. I'm here for you, whatever happens. I've got you."

Alex felt as drawn to Erin's strength as she always had. "I think," Alex spoke carefully, considering, "I think that for so many years, I kept everything so deeply buried. I was so tightly wound for so long. Since being with you, it's like I suddenly have you to lean on. I have your arms to collapse into and cry when everything feels too hard. I have felt so vulnerable lately. I can't decide if falling apart in your arms is making me weaker or stronger, but I know I couldn't have continued living indefinitely as I was."

"It's the same for me too, you know," said Erin. "You give your strength to me when I need it. You might not see it that way. You might see yourself as vulnerable, but I see you as so strong, Alex. Everybody underestimates what it means to be you. But I see it every day and I see the toll it takes on you.

I'm here to protect you and support you in everything, and together we can be stronger."

Alex smiled and nuzzled into Erin. "I feel like with you by my side, I can achieve anything."

Erin smiled at her. Her dark green eyes looked so much lighter in the sun, and her smile held all the warmth and love that Alex had craved her whole life.

Erin, I love you.

11

Erin spent every morning with Vic and Shimmer, preparing for the National Championships. She would have never believed that something like this could have happened so quickly. It seemed like anything was possible with a horse like Shimmer and a trainer like Vic. This morning, she had washed Shimmer down in the sunshine, following a successful morning of jumping. Vic had left and Erin was heading back to the castle to get showered and changed, before visiting a school with Alex.

Erin worried about Alex recently and the stress she was under. While she worried about Alex's safety every time they were out in public, she also worried about Alex's mental state. The threat to her life was weighing heavily on Alex. Seeing Annabelle Delacourt and having Annabelle tell Alex that she had always loved her, had shaken Alex up far more than it might previously have done. Erin sensed an anxiety in Alex, as though she were waiting for something bad to happen. Maybe on some level, she was.

Their recent public appearances had been uneventful. Erin had noticed protestors occasionally, but mostly she had noticed the doubling in size of Alex's security team. Erin had been trained to understand that in times of threat, the team tightens in, closer to the princess. Lately the team had felt so close, it was no wonder that Alex felt like she could barely breathe.

She still insisted on business as usual. When Erin got back to their rooms, Alex was in hair and makeup with Alicia, and Alicia was chatting away to her.

Erin smiled and acknowledged them both before heading to the bathroom. She could smell the unmistakable stink of horses on herself: that potent mix of their sweat, the haylage that they ate, and the ammonia from the urine in their stables.

Erin knew it was a scent that horsey people loved, but it wasn't a scent normal people wanted to smell. She shed her clothes, showered and dressed neatly for the day ahead.

Alex looked stressed this morning, but Erin couldn't pinpoint why. It was a beautiful summer morning and Alex loved the work she was doing in the schools. But even Audrey padded around the room, looking unsettled.

"Did someone take Audrey out?" Erin asked.

"Yes, I did, before Alicia got here. I don't know why she won't stop wandering around." Alex's bright blue eyes in the mirror were fixed on Erin.

Erin sat down and called Audrey over. "Hey, girl," she ruffled the short hair on the top of Audrey's head and looked into her big, wise eyes. "What is it, girl? You don't want your mums going out and leaving you again today? You'll be all right. Jess is going to take you to hang out with her today, and I'm sure she will take you for a nice walk later. You like Jess." Audrey thrust her massive head into Erin's hands. A Great Dane was a bold choice of dog, but it had always been Alex's ambition to have a Great Dane. She said castles were made for big dogs and a small dog would look tiny in the big rooms. And she had been right. Audrey fit perfectly into the castle and into their lives. Luckily, there was no shortage of staff to look after her when they were both out.

They headed out in the Range Rover to a school just north of London. As they drove around the M25, Erin couldn't stop herself from wondering what was going on with Alex.

"Lex, what's up? You aren't yourself today."

Alex looked contemplative for a minute. "I know. I wish I knew what was up with me. It's nothing. There is nothing wrong. I just have a bad feeling about today. I can't shake it."

"Based on anything?"

"No, nothing at all. Just a feeling."

"Then, it's nothing, Alex. There's nothing to worry about. We are all here to protect you. Nothing bad will happen."

Alex leaned into her. "I just want to continue our perfect lives and our perfect love without this shit hanging over us. I keep asking and they keep saying that they are investigating, and they promise they will figure it out. But nothing has been figured out. They are still telling me every day that there is a high threat level against me. Well, they don't even need to tell me. I feel it because of how close the team is to me. I feel it when I see the stressed looks on their faces. They think I don't notice, but I do. I feel every moment of them closing in around me."

"It won't go on forever, you know. They will find the source eventually. They will take whatever steps necessary to protect you. We've got each other and we will get through this together. We can get through anything together." Erin squeezed her hand and Alex smiled weakly.

"I love you."

"I love you, too." Erin kissed the top of her golden head. Despite everything, she felt lucky every second of every day to have found the kind of love she shared with Alex.

Soon, they arrived at the school. Normal for a mall-town visit, half the population had turned out to get a glimpse of Alex. There were hundreds of people cheering from behind barriers. They held Union Jack flags. They held photos of Erin and Alex. They held bunches of flowers for Erin and Alex. They held their phones high, hoping to capture video footage of Alex and Erin, and their visit to this small town.

Erin got out first and made her way to the other side of the vehicle, where Joanne was opening the door for Alex. Alex's lovely face was suddenly lit up brightly by the sun. Her smile was wide as she stepped down from the vehicle and waved happily at the people. Nobody else had any idea about the anxiety Alex had felt on the journey, but Erin could still see flashes of it. Small movements of fear across her eyes. Alex began to greet people warmly, to sign autographs, and to pose for photos. Erin went through the motions of mimicking Alex's public persona by smiling and signing and posing, but something felt different today. Was it Alex's anxiety? Was it getting to Erin?

Erin shook her head, trying to shake herself out of it. She stayed close to Alex and her eyes discretely darted around the area whenever she wasn't smiling, greeting, or signing.

Suddenly, there was something and Erin wasn't sure what it was. A flash of metal at the edge of her vision, a quick movement from the security team, a loud crack of a noise so unmistakable that it could only be a gunshot. She reacted instantly, throwing her body at Alex, wrapping her, engulfing her, throwing them both to the ground.

Screaming and chaos rang out all around them. Erin heard the security team shouting down their radios trying to take control of the situation. She heard Joanne's voice firm and in control, "There's a lot of blood. I think Rose is shot. Repeat,

Rose has been hit. We need to move her right now. Erin, move. ERIN, MOVE."

Rose, that is Alex's security codename. Rose is shot; Alex is shot.

She heard the crowds panicking. She heard Alex screaming underneath her. Erin felt herself being pulled from where she lay on top of Alex. She held on tightly and closed her eyes. She had to keep Alex safe.

12

Alex had seen the momentary panic in Erin's eyes before feeling the impact, as she was thrown to the ground with Erin on top of her. Then there was the chaos and the screaming. She heard Joanne saying, "Rose is hit."

Alex looked down at herself. She was wearing a white blouse and from what she could see, there was just blood. Was this what it felt like to be shot? She felt shocked, like she wasn't really there. Alex hadn't felt any pain and adrenaline coursed through her veins.

Erin was still on top of her. She felt somehow safe underneath Erin's reassuring weight. Joanne was trying to move Erin and pull her away, but Erin was clinging to Alex.

Quickly, more members of the security team were there to assist Joanne. They pulled Erin away from her and one of the big men scooped up Alex from the ground. "Where is the wound? Get her into the car. Get her the fuck out of here! Get pressure on the wound."

There was so much blood on her and Alex felt dazed and confused. The security team bundled her into the car.

Joanne's voice again. "Fuck, it's Erin. Sergeant Kennedy is shot. We have to go. We have to get Rose out of here."

Alex heard her own voice screaming, "Erin?! Erin! Oh my god!"

Alex tried to sit up on the back seat of the Range Rover, only to see Erin on the floor on the road outside in a pool of blood surrounded by security. The door was slammed and the Range Rover drove away quickly, with Alex screaming helplessly for Erin.

Alex felt strong arms around her as she sobbed helplessly. It was Joanne.

"Ma'am, Ma'am, stay calm. They are looking

after Erin. She will be taken straight to the hospital. Ma'am, let me look at you. Are you hit? Does it hurt anywhere? Please. Calm down."

Alex tried to stop, somewhat unsuccessfully. "I don't think I am hurt. I think it is Erin's blood." Alex felt her own torso with her fingers, testing the skin as if she might find vast gaping holes in her body. She found nothing. She could taste the iron of the blood in her mouth.

"Can I?" Joanne questioned, and Alex nodded. She felt Joanne's hands at the buttons of her blouse. Undoing them, wiping the blood from her skin, feeling for the injury that she had been so sure was there. Joanne threw a blanket over Alex.

She heard Joanne speaking into the microphone at her wrist again, "I don't think Rose was hit. I think it is Sergeant Kennedy's blood. Should we take Rose to the hospital to get checked or somewhere else?"

"Hospital. I demand you take me to Erin. That is an order." Alex felt suddenly adamant.

"We need to be sure she is okay. Take her to the hospital. We have mobilized a team. They will meet you at the entrance to the Accident and Emergency Department. We also have a top cardiothoracic surgeon flying in."

Alex closed her eyes. How could this be happening? Erin had to be okay. She had to be. Alex had thought long and hard about the risk to herself, but it had never crossed her mind that in selfishly pursuing the things that were important to her, she had also risked Erin's life. How could she have been so stupid? How did she think her bodyguards protected her? Why hadn't she insisted Erin that wore a Kevlar vest when they were out?

God, how could this be happening?

In the hospital, she kept asking to see Erin. But nobody would tell her anything. Joanne was by her side as she was whisked through to a private room.

"I'm Doctor Alison Chambers, Ma'am. It is a pleasure to meet you. I'm so sorry you have been through such a horrific ordeal. Would you mind if I had a good look at you, just to check you are okay?"

Alex nodded dully. "Joanne, can you *please* go and find out how Erin is? Or I'm walking out this door and going to find her myself."

"Ma'am, of course." Joanne walked to the

corner of the room. Alex should have known she wouldn't leave. Joanne used her radio and phone to find out the information Alex had demanded.

"Ma'am, are you feeling any pain anywhere?"

Only my heart, thought Alex. "No, not really. I think I hit the back of my head when I fell to the ground. It is a bit sore. But, no."

The doctor began to remove Alex's clothes so she could examine her. After she was done, she asked if Alex might want to shower and directed her to a small room off the corner of the room they were in.

Alex headed to the bathroom and caught sight of herself in the mirror. No wonder they wanted her to shower. She was covered in blood. All over her face, in her hair, across her chest. Her blouse had been soaked in blood when they took it off her.

Erin's blood.

Alex began to sob, showering quickly. The hot water cleansed her and brought her back to life.

How do I live without Erin? She's dead, isn't she? Nobody loses that much blood and is fine. That is why they won't tell me anything. How am I supposed to go on without her?

"Ma'am, Sergeant Kennedy is in surgery." Dr Chambers spoke to her calmly. "She has a penetrating wound by a bullet to the left side of her body. It has done some damage to her pulmonary artery and has lodged inside her body. The surgeons are working now to remove it and to try and repair the damage."

"Will she die?" Alex asked, calmly. "Do not bullshit me because of who I am. I need you to be absolutely honest with me here. What are her chances?"

"Ma'am, honestly, I don't know. She is young and she is healthy, but she has lost a lot of blood. Sometimes injuries like these have bad outcomes. Sometimes they have good outcomes."

"By 'bad outcomes,' you mean death?"

"Yes, Ma'am, by 'bad outcome' I mean death. It is possible, but not definite. Your people have flown in Dr. Karala, and she is the best cardiothoracic surgeon in the country. If you could choose anyone you could have to perform this surgery, it would be Dr Karala."

Alex sobbed quietly into the hospital gown she was now wearing.

"Ma'am." It was Joanne, touching Alex's wrist tenderly. "They want to move you somewhere safer, but I told them it was very unlikely you would agree to leave the hospital with Erin in surgery."

"Thank you, Joanne," Alex found herself mumbling. "I'm not going anywhere without her."

"Right, so in that case I have sent for some clothes to be brought for you. I have also sent for Victoria Grey-Hughes. And Prince Nicolas is still in London, and has asked to come and sit with you. You can have either or both of them, but I figured you might want someone with you right now."

Alex smiled, thinly. "Thank you, Joanne."

Alex sat between the much bigger figures of Nicolas and Vic in the hospital's family room. Their size felt like protection for her from the world right now. All she could think about was Erin, who had been in surgery for hours. Alex rested her head on Vic's shoulder and Nicolas held her hand. A bag of Haribo gummies rested on her lap and a plastic cup of rapidly cooling hot, sweet tea sat by her feet. Vic said she needed sugar at a time like this.

Alex thought about how before Erin, she had had no close friends, but in allowing herself to open up to Erin, she had also allowed herself to become friends with Vic and Nicolas. Erin had brought them to her, and now they were holding her together while she waited for news about Erin.

Please don't die, Erin. You have to come back to me.

Dr Karala was a small woman with dark hair and smooth brown skin. She may have been small, but like Alex, she knew how to command attention. Her presence, as she glided into the room for families, immediately drew everyone's eyes. Her surgical gown made her look like a goddess. *The goddess with the power to save lives*, Alex thought.

"Ma'am, Princess Alexandra, I am Josephine Karala. I have worked on your partner, Erin."

"Is she alive? Please tell me, I have to know." Alex felt utter desperation.

"She is alive. I removed the bullet. I also

repaired significant damage to her pulmonary artery. She is in recovery now. We can't say anything for sure right now, but the surgery went as well as we could have hoped for, and her body is doing well so far. All being well, she should make a full recovery in time."

Alex jumped up and threw her arms around the surprised surgeon. "Thank you so very much. As well as saving her life in the OR, you have saved mine too. Can I see her? I'll just sit with her quietly? Please? I need this so very much."

Alex's eyes met the eyes of the surgeon.

"Okay, but she won't wake for a while. You must just sit quietly with her. Her body has been through a huge amount of stress. She will need time and peace to recover."

"Take me to her, please."

Security swarmed as Alex got up to move. She didn't care this time. She was going to Erin. Erin was going to be okay.

Alex didn't know what she was expecting, but she gasped audibly as she saw Erin. Big, strong Erin looking suddenly small in a hospital bed. In a hospital gown. Hooked up to machinery. Alex moved to the side of the bed and sat quietly next to the woman she loved. She took Erin's hand in her own smaller one and traced lines across it with her fingers.

She settled to wait and watch Erin.

Please be ok. Please be ok. Please be ok.

Rob Greene appeared at the window to Erin's room and signaled to her. Alex went outside, never taking her eyes off Erin, to hear what he had to say. "Ma'am, we have the shooter in custody. We also have the people he was involved with, the people who were funding the protesters. It was all done with the aim of getting the king's brother to ascend the throne after him. We are further investigating Prince Arthur's possible involvement in this plot. Anyway, I thought you would want to know. It's over now. The threat to your life is over."

Alex breathed out the breath she hadn't realized she had been holding. "Thank you, Rob. Good work."

"Ma'am, please give my best to Sergeant Kennedy. She has gone above and beyond any duty, and without doubt, she saved your life today. She is a hero."

Alex smiled. "I know. I will be eternally grateful to her. Thank you, Rob."

"Thank you, Ma'am."

13

When Erin opened her eyes, the first thing she saw was Alex's lovely face and the concern in her eyes.

"You're alive," Erin mumbled.

"Of course I'm alive," Alex smiled. "It's you who got shot!"

"Really?" Erin murmured. "There was so much blood. On your shirt. I was so sure they had got you."

"I am absolutely fine, I promise you that." Alex squeezed her hand.

"So I got shot? Am I okay?"

"You've had surgery and they've fixed you up. They think you will be okay. Just got to take it easy while you recover. Rob Greene said they had caught everyone involved in it and that there is no longer a threat on my life. It is over. You saved my life, you know? You threw me to the ground to save me. You put your body between me and the bullet."

"Well, that's my job." Erin tried to laugh, but it hurt.

"Not anymore, silly. You are my girlfriend now, remember? Not my protector." Alex smiled at her.

"I'll always be your protector, Princess Alexandra."

The next day, Erin felt a little better, but god, it hurt where she had been shot! Alex still hadn't left her bedside. Instead, she had slept in the chair next to Erin's bed. Alex had washed her body tenderly and carefully as she lay in the bed.

Erin found herself falling asleep again in the afternoon. Her body must have needed the sleep to heal.

When she woke, it was evening, and she saw the sun setting through the window. Alex was still sitting next to her, looking contemplative and effortlessly lovely with the red and orange backdrop of the sky. Erin had tried half-heartedly to make her leave and go and get some food and sleep, but she had refused. Erin knew that Alex wouldn't leave her because if it had been the other way around, she wouldn't have left Alex.

"So, I was thinking," Alex began. "I love you, Erin Kennedy. You saved my life yesterday, but you save my life every day. You have helped me find myself. The self I had buried so deeply that I had forgotten it even existed. I owe you absolutely everything. I can't wait for our future together. And, I was just wondering," Alex paused for a second to look into Erin's eyes. "Will you marry me?"

Erin felt her eyes widen in shock. She loved Alex unreservedly and she knew she wanted nothing more, but she had never imagined that marriage could be a reality for them. There were so many complications.

"Um, you think that is possible?"

"Anything is possible, particularly when my dad is the king. Now please, for god's sake, answer the question!"

Erin's answer was instinctual and without any doubt.

"Yes. A thousand times, yes. I want to spend the rest of forever loving you."

Alex smiled and leaned in and kissed her gently.

Alex produced a bag of Haribo gummies. She had one of those looks on her face. "So, I want to give you a ring that was my grandmother's. It is stunning, but I don't have it here. So, I was thinking this ring might do until we get home." She produced a gummy ring from the Haribo bag and slid it onto the fourth finger on Erin's left hand. "Sergeant Erin Kennedy, will you be my wife?"

Erin laughed and it hurt. She admired the ring on her left hand. "This is beautiful, Alex. Is there another one in that bag? I think you should wear one too."

Alex dug through the bag and found another gummy ring, which she put on her own left hand, laughing because it was too big on her delicate finger.

Erin smiled at her fiancée. She wasn't sure how their marriage would happen, but she knew damn well that Alex would make it a reality.

Erin had had all these vivid dreams while she had been unconscious, convinced that Alex had been shot, that Alex was dead, that she would lose Alex.

But upon waking, here was Alex, lovely and so very much alive. Alex would be her wife someday soon.

Erin felt happiness deep inside her.

Today was the beginning of the rest of their lives together.

I want to spend the rest of forever loving you.

BOOK 3
FOREVER WITH A PRINCESS

Alexandra and Erin's wedding will be the first ever Royal Wedding between two women.

It soon transpires that there is a group of people working to not let the wedding happen. When things start to get tense amongst close family and friends, who exactly can they trust?

Alexandra and Erin are perfect for each other.

Will they get to walk down the aisle in the end?

getbook.at/HRB3

Printed in Dunstable, United Kingdom